Orkney

Orkney

AMY SACKVILLE

COUNTERPOINT
BERKELEY

Supported using public funding by the National Lottery
through Arts Council England

Library of Congress Cataloging-in-Publication data is available.

ISBN 978-1-61902-119-8

COUNTERPOINT
1919 Fifth Street
Berkeley, CA 94710
www.counterpointpress.com

Printed in the United States of America
Distributed by Publishers Group West

10 9 8 7 6 5 4 3 2 1

For my grandparents, Nancy and Joseph

. . . the portrait of a story attacked from all sides, that attacks itself and in the end gets away.

Hélène Cixous, Stigmata

'Oh, she'll be back. That dear one
Is gold of our corn,
She's Orkney rain and spindrift . . .'

George Mackay Brown,
'Gossip in Hamnavoe: About a Girl'

Sunday

She's staring out to sea now. My young wife. There she stands on the barren beach, all wrapped up in her long green coat, among the scuttle and clatter of pebbles and crabs. She stares out as the water nears her feet and draws back, and when that soft and insistent suck of the tide gets close enough to slurp at her toes she shuffles herself up the shore. Soon the beach will be reduced to a strip of narrow sand and she will be forced to retreat to the rocks; and then, I think, she'll come back to me.

In the meantime, I watch from the window, as she stares out to sea.

Where shall I take you, I asked, when we are wed? 'The sea,' she answered. 'Will you take me to the sea?' Oh, I said grandly, oh I will pour out oceans for you. I will take you to the vast Pacific calm, California, Japan; or to the warm waters that Asia cradles; Indian, Atlantic, which would you like? We can go to the centre of the old known world, sail the wine-dark seas Odysseus sailed and lose ourselves among the islands, and in the evenings we'll come ashore and eat on a terrace by the beach, simply and well, with our fingers. We'll swim together naked in the last of the sun, as the long day sets, like innocents . . . But at this, her patient smile was frozen and she stopped me, horrified. 'No, no,' she said. 'I won't go *in*. I can't swim. I'm scared of the water. I can't go in.'

I kissed her head, smoothed her smooth white hair. Well then, wherever you want, I said, undeterred; we'll seek out the softest snowy sands of the tropics, and you can lay out upon them, paler still; or we'll float upon the surface of the Dead Sea and let salt leach our skins and have no fear of sinking; or we'll sail the unfathomed fjords in the chill dawn, and admire their depths from the safety of the deck; wherever you wish, that's where we'll go. 'North,' she said, 'take me north.' Very well, I said, with a deep bow that she laughed at, with a courtly kiss of her fingers; if that be your bidding. Where the waves rush in iron-grey and unforgiving, like the cavalry of old wars. Very well. North.

She was born here, she says, on one of these tiny ragged islands. But she says nothing remains of her father's family, and she left when she was still a child, crossed the strait and moved south of the border; and when we came to choose our Orkney she couldn't say which it was she hailed from. And so, trusting to predestination, eschewing tourist offices, internet searches and travel guides, she took a pin and, eyes screwed tight shut and neck straining to prove that her head was turned, circled above the map laid out on the table and without hesitation came down on our chosen isle, our fate decided by a child's game or a witch at play. Not once, I think, did she fear that she might plunge us into the ocean with that gull's dive of her pointed hand; it did not occur to her that she might miss land altogether and send us smashing into the waves, forced to make our honeymoon among the seals and the fishes. Her aim was unerring, and with that blind leap she brought us here, to surely the loneliest, the rockiest, the most desolate island that has yet been mapped, in this or any other water. The rusted mauve of the flattened flora, the dark grasses on the tree-less earth. And this house just as she hoped for, on an unsheltered shore, creaking and rattling and whistling with the wind off the sea, whispering and moaning. A hulking ghost of another island somewhere in the mist to the west, and looking out to the north, nothing but the bird-scattered, crashing ocean, and beyond to where it meets the sky; a line called the hilder, she says, in these parts; a line sometimes luminous, sometimes obscure.

Just as she is – luminous, obscure. There she stands.

Yesterday morning, at home, I woke beside her for the first time. Well, that is not quite true; last night I slept beside her for the first time, but by dawn I had woken beside her a dozen times, a hundred times, sometimes from a sleep so shallow I couldn't call it waking. Again and again I turned to find another body in my bed, an unfamiliar warmth alongside my own, and wondered where I was and what I had done, before remembering and sinking again into a grateful doze – only to wake again moments later. Each time, as the brown abstraction of my surroundings resolved into the ordinary shapes of my own bedroom, there was still that body beside me, a living residue of an impossibly optimistic dream. All night, the rise and fall of her form, the snuffle and snore. Once, she muttered something I couldn't understand; she muttered and rolled and even giggled, twice. A secret amusement, a private joke. She slept with the covers pulled to her chin. And finally, I checked the bedside clock and there was only ten minutes before the alarm was due to sound. I watched the little frowns that crossed her brow, pale in that colourless hour before dawn; the pucker at the corners of her lips, the halting sigh of her dreaming. I wanted to let her sleep on, this stranger in my bachelor's double bed, sagging on one side from too many years of unequal use, the other half buoyant under her body. But it couldn't be helped; we were to rise early to catch our train. I switched off the alarm before it rang, and woke her gently a few minutes later, with a kiss and a cup of tea ready and a whisper in her ear. Time to get up, Mrs _____.

'Good morning, Professor,' she mumbled. What were you

dreaming? I asked, sitting on the bed and stroking her hair back. She turned her face up from the pillow, rubbed a wrist across her nose and eyes like a child, bleary, surfacing, accepting the cup with a smile. 'Jellyfish, I think,' she murmured. 'Lots of jellyfish. All pale and round like fringed moons. I was floating in among them. They were tickling.' Ah, that was it, I said, that was what made you laugh. 'Did I?' she said; and then, suddenly accusatory: 'Was it *you*? Tickling?' I? No! I replied, mock-innocent; in truth I wish it had been, and not some lunar interloper, slinking over her unconscious skin. Pulsing and falling all about her, the silver tendrils of her hair twining with theirs. I can't bear to cede even an inch of her in flesh or thought, now that I have her; it seems cruel that there should be these unconscious hours that I can take no part in. How ridiculous, to envy this flotilla of dream-figments. This fluther. She taught me the word; I suspect her of making it up. She swears it is true. 'A whole fluther of them,' she said. She was delighted to have remembered it; it pleased her all the way to the station, a little tickled smile playing over her mouth, a little giggle as I tickled in the back of the taxi.

Shall I sneak out there now, over the rocks and onto the beach, sneak up behind her and tickle her? But perhaps her mood has changed. I can't tell if she wants to be alone or if she's hoping I might join her. I haven't yet learned how to gauge the hours apart. We've been happily trammelled up together for two days now. It's possible she wants a little solitude.

She keeps a safe distance between herself and the water; but sometimes a wave will surprise her, building under the surface and suddenly breaking tall just as it comes to the beach and making a grab for her, and then she leaps back and stands a little further off. I cannot tell from here, from the angle of her head, if she is curious, amused, watchful, thoughtful, thoughtless. Not a thought in her head, perhaps, just the sound of the sea, just the wash and glint of it.

We came to our island by land, by air, by sea, setting out early on the east coast route to Edinburgh. She grew quiet on the train as we left the gentler moors behind us, her forehead resting against the window. As we passed through Northumberland, her mother's country, I watched her eyes skitter as her gaze caught and was repeatedly torn from some stricken root or crag or hollow. This hard, sparse corner of England she once called home. She left for the last time this summer and has no intention of going back, she says. I asked if she misses it, but she didn't answer, only looked out as if at any moment her ancestral queens would breast a ridge and ride out of the blue mist; whether wistful or apprehensive I couldn't determine, having only the curve of her turned cheek to go on.

She was quiet, too, as we made our way through the airport; we were, I think, a little shy of each other. There are so many of these commonplace rituals we have yet to share. For my part, wishing to seem at ease, well-travelled, adept in the shedding of jacket and belt, the flip of identification, the casual presentation of boarding pass. Perhaps she felt the same. Perhaps she had some other reason to be pensive. I found myself unable to ask, or to reassure her; we seemed exposed, unreal, or too real, in the shadowless glare. I kept a hand on the small of her back and guided her, unspeaking, through the terminal until we reached the deserted departure lounge, at the furthest end of the building. She was smiling but preoccupied as we made our way onto the tiny plane and held my hand with quick, nervous glances at the three other passengers, all travelling alone, all keeping to themselves; two wiry middle-aged women and a stocky blond man with a reddish beard, his face set, it seemed to me, in a permanent, averted leer. I made sure we sat behind him, and away from all eyes. On the runway, accelerating, I felt the tendons of her wrist wind tighter until I thought she might snap beside me; as we left the ground she let out a breath, kissed me, and whispered excitedly, 'Orkney!'

Once airborne, she became animated, chattering and charming, looking out of the window and turning to me to exclaim over what she saw — I barely know what it was that so thrilled her, her low voice muted by the loud whirr of the turbines. But I watched her and I felt the grip of her hand on my wrist, and lip-read a discourse on firths and mountains, I think, on low and highlands, snow and islands . . . and I circled the pit of her palm with my fingers and watched her mouth moving, absorbed in the bite and flash of her teeth, quite disregarding the view. And at last I could not resist bending to her ear to ask, are you happy? She drew back, beaming, leaned in to reply: 'Happy? I'm exulting.' Effervescing. Jubilant. 'I'm in raptures,' she cried, 'I'm rapturous. I am,' she said, with a gesture at the window and the bright silken skeins of cirrus below, 'as they say, on cloud nine.' And low in my ear, a murmur against my jawbone: 'Ecstatic.' I conceded the game, I could think of no better word. I wonder, is there any word at all to come near her? She looked back to the window and I watched her, ecstatic, as we began to descend over a jigsaw scatter of low-lying islands.

At the Mainland harbour we found a little ferryboat with a captain who would take us to our own island, the last leg of our long journey, as the wintry sun was sinking. A thin, gaunt man with a gloomy demeanour, and the darkness of the ocean in his glower. As I talked, he kept his eyes on my wife; she, in turn, seemed to subject him to a subtle scrutiny, from lowered blue lids. I showed him our map, described the cottage on the shore, hoping that he might be willing to take us to this end of the known earth. 'Aye, the noust hoose, ah know it,' he said, as if many others had ventured there before us. Which I find impossible to believe is true.

He peered at her face as he helped her on board – my bold lass barely faltering, and not looking down. She was wearing a hat, pulled low, her hair tucked up in it. 'Is this yir dochter?' he asked. My wife, I said, she is my wife. Only yesterday, she stood at my side and gave her hand, and we emerged together into a cold, bright October afternoon, I raffishly resplendent in my old tux, she shivering in silk. How lovely she was in the autumn light, her skin opalescent, her clavicle sharp with the cold that tensed her shoulders, and a flush on her chest despite it; her hair ablaze in the sun. Her silver head beside my grey one. I imagined the people passing on the pavement, in cars, thinking us a sweet old couple, catching a better glimpse as they drew near enough to make her out and puzzling over it as they went by. I held her closer and indulged a gloat. No family on either side. Mine all gone, hers uninvited, and all mention avoided; her father wasn't there to give her away. He gave her away long ago, she says. But no matter. We have no need for others, now.

I said nothing of all this to the boatman. I said simply, she is my wife. At this, his tremendous eyebrows, which swept like the wings of a great seabird over his forehead, almost touched his hairline. She smiled her most glittering smile, and I thought I caught for a moment, in the flash of his glare, a lust as if he coveted the silver in her eyes. But then, he turned back to his boat with a frown, tamping his pipe with a jab of his square-tipped finger. A pipe, I thought. Of course. Why not.

And it should not surprise me, his taciturn censure; how we must look, after all. I towering, twice her size across the shoulders, cragged and steel-grey; she almost as tall but so slight and young, so strange and pale. Her unlined face turned to me, attending only to me; doting, even. As absorbed as she ever was in the lecture hall, and I proud and perhaps a little proprietary. Ours is a marriage of minds, I wanted to tell him. But why should I feel the need to excuse it? She is a grown woman. If she can see past the forty years between us – almost forty, not quite – if she can love me for them, even, and not in spite, then the rest of the world can go blind, for all that it matters to me.

She wears both rings on a chain about her neck, hidden under shirt and jumper and high-buttoned coat collar – a diamond solitaire and a silver band. Both were slipped on with great ceremony, and slipped off again as soon, I think, as it seemed polite to do so. She apologises. It is uncomfortable, she says, for her to wear a ring. She splays her hand; between each of those narrow, knuckly, fine-tapered fingers, there is a trace of webbing. A blue-veined membrane stretched between. You were born for the sea, I tell her. 'And yet I can't swim.'

So I bought her a silver chain, and so it is that my wife goes into the world unbanded on my arm, which lends credence to the common assumption that she is my maligned, molested daughter, not my spouse; and I am a monster to flaunt it in their faces . . . well, she is not my daughter, and she is a grown woman, and I shall flaunt it and be damned. I tilted her chin up and kissed her; I kissed her neck, her collarbone, and nuzzled up under the rim of her hat to kiss the hidden place behind her ear, and we tangled into a knot of limbs and scarves and twining fingers. I cast a glance at our captain. Ours is a marriage of minds, indeed, but of much else besides, I thought. Put that in your pipe and smoke it.

He cast off and I felt the grip of those dear webbed fingers on my sleeve, and the other hand twisted through mine as if she'd break it, and she stood there at the rail, rigid, and stared straight ahead to the horizon, not looking down. Her pointed pale profile and her hair escaping, strands of it whipping in the wind, and her eyes wide like whirlpools; and I imagined some Kraken, dripping slime and black ooze and sea-wrack, roaring out of his deep green sunken grotto to claim her. These pen-and-ink visions, an illustration from some glossy colour plate; she could be lifted out of my library. She infects me with a fin-de-siècle fever, her streaming eyes, bloodless cheeks, high colour rising at the temples.

After half an hour, we began to list and rock, the sea heaving under us and shrugging us off; the light that seeped through the layered cloud from the setting sun was a late, jaundiced yellow. 'Yin's a skyuimy lift, aye,' said our captain, nodding at the sky. 'Is yir yink trowie?' I begged his pardon. 'The wife. She's no weel,' he translated; and it was true that her face, in that light, had a sickly hue. 'I'm fine,' she said through clenched jaw, lips set in a grim line, her eyes fixed on the island that was at last approaching. A solid mass of black, emerging from the glinting darkness of the water. We rounded a high headland and came to the northern shore; a few sparse-spread yellow lights beckoning, offering warmth and sanctuary, and one of them our own. And so we arrived at our honeymoon island, bidding farewell to the captain and stepping unsteadily on to the little dock as the evening purpled into gloaming, a slip of crescent moon rising, and the boat roared off until the sound of the waves drowned the engine. And then the sea was all that we could hear, and she assured me she felt better, and we stood for a moment listening in the violet darkness, and then raggled up the beach, ready for bed after a long day's journeying. Despite her brave insistence that she would not stumble, I lifted her and carried her to the door triumphant, revelling in her lightness and my own abiding strength. New wives, after all, must be lifted over the threshold. Like witches, so I'm told. She is an endlessly fascinating fund of such trivia.

We were met at the cottage, as promised, by a Mrs Odie. Her bright wind-hardened eyes had tracked our progress. 'Just a peedie lassie . . .' she muttered as we drew nearer; I growled under my breath a little, feeling the pin-pricks of her peering as she moved aside to let us in. An old Orkney woman with the face of a weather-beaten bannock, and that gimlet stare out of poked holes in the dough. I set my wife down over the threshold, and she followed us in what I took to be mute moral outrage. But after all, the fire was lit, and there was brisket and bread and thick warm lentil soup, and her exit was gracious enough in her own stumping way. And then we were left alone.

My wife looked at me solemnly then, her hands in a prayer over mine; and then with a little leap, turned tail and pelted down the hallway, into the kitchen and out the other side, bounced once on the sofa and up and off she went again, leaving no impression behind; I followed her round and about, tracking her, like a dog sniffing after traces, room after room, hunting through the house. I caught up to her in the bedroom at last, panting and pretending I wasn't breathless, listening for her, knowing she was in there although I couldn't see her. I caught a brief gleam in a looking-glass and she leapt on me from behind the door and I snatched her up, and for the second time in our married life, I laid her down.

I put my tongue to the palm of my hand now and think I can still taste her, the salty tang of her skin. I look out to where she stands and, for just a moment, she glances back at the house shyly. She makes no gesture. The sun is low, it fills the window, and perhaps from beyond she cannot see me for its glare.

Later in the evening I brought out the champagne that I had carried all that way; train-rattled, air-pressured, sea-rolled, it opened with an irrepressible pop and spill, into the tumblers that were all I could find in the cupboard. She curled up on the sheep-skin before the fire, and I took my seat beside her gamely, with a gamey crack of the knees, stiff from a day of sitting. And we toasted each other and polished off the bottle with some thick beef sandwiches in quiet, travel-worn contentment; and she went off to the bathroom to wash and brush her teeth, and I enjoyed the fire a little longer, pouring myself a dram from my flask and savouring the spice of it, feeling the heat of it over my chest, and deeper in me the warmth of anticipation. But when I went into the bedroom she smiled drowsily out of the burrow of blankets she'd made about herself, and by the time I returned from my own ablutions, she was quite, quite asleep, and so sweetly that I couldn't wake her, despite my want.

But a few hours later she woke anyway, shocking me into consciousness with a great and frightening gasp as if she had been hauled from the depths. She dreamt of a deluge, she said, and she was drenched by it. Her gown stuck to her damp skin, her face shining in the dark. She said she'd dreamt that she stood on a high cliff, and as she looked down she saw the water rushing back, and the shells and the jellyfish and the urchins and the skeletons, whales and ships and men, all bleached to bone, all exposed on the sandy seabed, the sea pulling back for miles and miles; and then gathering, mounting, as if some invisible giant had rolled it all back like a carpet, and then let go. She saw it rushing towards her, tumbling over and over itself, and pushing all the bones and waste and wreck before it, smashing against the cliff she stood on, and she felt the spray of it, she saw it rushing up the wall of rock, and just as it breached the edge, just as it hit her, she woke with that gasp, as if it had knocked the breath out of her.

I held her by the shoulders and promised she was safe, but she wouldn't meet my eye; she went on staring out to the sea that still assailed her in the darkness. So I pulled her to me, and felt her ribcage hard against my side, and still she would not look at me; I covered her cheek with my hand and she allowed her face to be turned, passive as I kissed her, grasped her, eased her rigid body back upon the bed and covered it with mine, seeking out her frightened eyes, which stared and stared beyond me as if she couldn't quite surface. And then at last she let them close and held to me as if for life.

What is it that makes her cling so? I have perfect circular bruises on my arms and thighs from her fingers and heels, and pressing them now, matching my fingertips to the blue shadows of hers, I know she loves me. She's told me as much. Looking out at her there at the tidemark, and looking down at the paling grey hairs, the dry skin of my forearms, I wish I had something more than a bruise and her word. But it seems there is no other convincing explanation.

This morning, our first on the island, I left her sleeping; the blind, which I was sure I had lowered before getting into bed, was open to the dawn, so that I had the impression of waking very early, and rose with a sense of vigour as I went about the making of coffee, the slicing and toasting of bread. And only when I glanced at the kitchen clock, as she wandered in rubbing still-sleepy eyes, did I see that it was past nine; how far we have turned from the sun, so far north. How long the nights. Hello sleepyhead, I said, kissing the pale pink skin just visible at the centre of her crown. How are you this morning?

'Such a strange dream,' she yawned; 'of a tidal wave, and the beach was all covered in bones . . .' And she told me the dream over, as if she had no recollection of waking and telling me in the night, as if I had not held her as she shivered, as if I had not warmed her, as if she had not even woken when I, when we, when she . . . well.

That gasp of hers.

She sat at the table, ruffling her hair into a fluffed cloud, squeezing shut her eyes as if to clear them of salt water, rubbing her fair brows into disorder with strong fingertips, and then looked up at me apparently revived. I felt a rush of fondness, then, for a morning ritual that I could already imagine watching and still adoring, years hence; the sight of my wife rejoining the world.

Mrs Odie had provided butter and milk, and I found marmalade in a cupboard, left by a previous guest I suppose, with a quaint hand-written label, possibly decades old, possibly an antique. Do you think this will be okay? I asked. 'It's a preserve,' she said. 'Clue's in the name.' But surely even preserves must moulder? She put out her hand for it, twisted the lid, the sinew of her wrist tautening to turn it, sniffed inside. 'I should say well-preserved. Mature.' Pungent? I said. 'Ripe,' she said, reassuringly. She cut a chunk of cold butter and mashed the surface of her toast with it, trying to spread the unspreadable, and slathered on the dark, bitter unguent from the jar, and pulled the rags of this mess to bits with her fingers and ate it at the window, taking small bites from first one torn half, then the other, dropping crumbs into the sink and looking out.

'I'm very pleased with our island. Do you think it's cold outside?' she asked. 'Shall we go for a walk?' Yes, let's, I said. I'll just wash up. I could make us a thermos. 'I can do that,' she said, 'you made the toast . . .' But she was already pulling her boots on eagerly. Go ahead, I said. I'll catch up. So she kissed me stickily, dark and bitter, rich and sweet, wrapped herself in her green coat and a green shawl, and went.

I saw her walk into the morning's thinning mist, down to the rocks that edge the sand, rising in a series of green-slippery black slabs. Undaunted, she hitched her skirt and made her way across them, carefully planting one foot at a time and testing it would hold before shifting weight on to it. I saw her bend down and pick up some sort of stick, washed up from some distant, arboreal shore, an anomaly; she looked back to the window and waved, gestured for me to come out and join her, swept a hand to encompass the sea, the shore, the rock-pools around her. She hunkered down, peering into the clear water; I saw her poke at something.

By the time I'd made a flask of tea and found a jumper in the pile of clothes she'd upended from our shared suitcase, she had reached the beach; it was low tide, the coarse white sand glowing faintly in the wan sun. She linked my arm and led me along the shore, swinging her legs so her long skirt swooshed about them, carefree. I asked her to tell me of her investigations. She'd found an anemone, she said, like a pale pink chrysanthemum. Is that what you were prodding at, I said, the poor creature, and she reddened, because she hadn't wanted to tell me the ugly part. 'Yes,' she said, 'but then it sucked into itself, all the petals folded and it looked like' – she blushed deeper and said quietly – 'a bottom.' Quite right, I said. It excretes from whence it eats. It has an arse for a mouth, and vice versa, I said. I meant to make her laugh but she looked so disappointed and I haven't since seen her poking with her stick.

At the end of the bay we circled back and, drawing level with the house, she sat down, looked up at me, and patted the sand beside her. So I sat. I poured out tea and handed a cup to her and nestled contentedly until the cold seemed to seep into me from under, my fingers growing stiff and toes numb in my brogues; she showed no signs of feeling it. I shivered. Shall we . . . I started to say, but she spoke at the same time: 'Are you cold? You should go in, you have work to do. You don't need to keep me company,' she said, 'I won't stay out long,' and she was smiling and she squeezed my gloved hand with her bare one kindly but nonetheless, it seemed I was dismissed.

No matter; I am content to watch her, here at the big picture window; my joints I fear are anyway too old for the haar. Oh, very well, I exaggerate. But I cannot deny the faintest senescent ache.

It is not the honeymoon I might have imagined, perhaps, once upon a time. If I ever imagined such a thing at all; certainly in recent years it hasn't crossed my mind. It is not the honeymoon I would have imagined someone of her age would imagine, either. But it was she who asked to come here, after all, and she says she's pleased to be here, and with me. And it is cosy in the tattered chair that I have pulled to the window, and I have been reading, working, making notes; a series of index cards, a pile of books, poring over illustrations in muted storm and woodland hues. I am writing a book of enchantment. Not, that is, a spell-book, a grimoire, not some leather-bound and gold-tooled tome with a creaking spine, but rather a work of academia – the culmination of a long career. It has been a long time in the making, this book, a long time promised. Just because we are on honeymoon, I can't neglect the terms of my sabbatical; it was all arranged before I even met her, and I have a deadline to keep and much to do before the spring. I tell her I hate to neglect her. She says she doesn't mind. There's the rest of the world to think of, she says, a sweet exaggeration. In fact she's delighted, can't wait to read it; she's read all my books, or so she says. I like to think of her with a stack of them, curled up snugly in a carrel in some dim corner of the library, underlining. And now I am drawing it all together into one great compendium, all the strands of forty years' thought: enchantment narratives in the nineteenth century. Transformations, obsessions, seductions; succubi and incubi; entrapments and escapes. The angel in the house become the maiden in the tower, the curse come upon her. Curses and cures. Folktales and fairy-tales retold. And all the attendant uncertainties, anxieties, and aporia. Do I wake or sleep? Fantasy and phantasm. Beautiful terrible women. Vulnerable lonely cursed women. Strange and powerful women. It's an old obsession. I still remember those first febrile encounters: propped up in the corner of my bed, scribbling away late into the night, in the old cheap editions I still have somewhere. And I have never outgrown that undergraduate ardour – Lamia, La Belle Dame, the Lady of Shalott. 'Always the women,' she says. I'm afraid so, I say. Her precedents.

If I am to spend some of these precious hours of our honeymoon lost in stories, drifting through myths and listening for echoes, then I could hardly have asked for a better retreat. This place not quite certainly present in either sense, this place of mists and changes, the barren scrubland, the wild sea – yes, it seems fitting, to do this work here. I believe it will be a very suitable, very comfortable arrangement. Glad of the peace, dozing a little, I woke up forty minutes ago befuddled, to find the sun already setting. And she is still staring out. And so I have turned away from my work, just for a moment, to attend to her. All those subtle serpents and slippery fishtailed maidens I have been trying to get hold of; for now it seems foolish to labour over fairy-tales when out there on the shore I have one of my own. I sit quietly here, adding to my endless index of her, observing as she becomes a silhouette.

She is Protean, a Thetis, a daughter of the sea, a shape-shifting goddess who must be subdued; I hold her fast and she changes, changes in my grasp . . . But I am no prince and cannot over-whelm her; she will consent to marry but goes on shifting no matter how tight I grip. Her hair falling like a torrent of water in which her fingers flick and twist. I dabble in her shallows and long to dive the depth of her.

She is a tiny, perfect, whittled trinket found bedded in the sand, carved patiently, for comfort; she is a spined and spiky urchin with an inside smooth as polished stone, as marble; she is a frond of pallid wrack, a coral swaying in the current, anchored to the sea-bed; she is an oyster, choking on grit, clutching her pearl to her.

She was my most gifted student, and now she is my wife.

And now, as promised and against all odds, she is returning; and so, I hope, soon to bed.

Monday

This morning again I woke before her; and again, the blind was
open, revealing a chalk-blue sky, a powdery opaque light dusting
the sea and her body. The blanket of her swaddled sleep discarded,
she lay flat on her back, limbs sprawled, and quite naked, defenceless, washed ashore and barely breathing. Her breasts flat against
her chest, the dip of her breast bone between them; the ridge of
each rib; her hips jutting, casting the faintest lilac shadows on her
skin in the pallid morning. A bruise by her hip, as if a thumb had
pressed into its hollow. I wondered how it got there. She bruises
easily, she says. Her palms turned up and curled gently, as if they
had lately released something precious. The high flat plains of
her Nordic face. The brows so fair they're almost invisible, like
an animal's fur, bunching thicker there on the bone. A faint, faint
snore.

'Are you awake?' she asked in the night. I wasn't quite, but I
heard her; she called me out of my sleep.

What is it? I said, reaching a hand behind me to grasp for
her. Can't sleep?

'I had another dream,' she said. 'That the cliff was leaking. I was standing on the beach below and the sea was glittering and the face of the cliff was running with waterfalls . . . but then I heard a crack, and I saw a massive seam opening in the rock, and the water rushed through and caught me, I couldn't keep my feet beneath me and I had to struggle up out of it and as I came up I saw the whole cliff, the whole island crumbling, all pouring on top of me like an avalanche of water.'

And then?

'I woke up. Or I drowned. Both.'

I squeezed again at her thigh; I said there won't be any drowning here. She was silent. I asked what is it, what is it you're afraid of? Why are you scared of the water? And she mumbled something I couldn't understand and I said I promise, I won't let you drown, and was on the point of turning to gather her into me but then, to my surprise (for I had imagined her to be an independent sleeper, as I am), she moved in towards me closer still and curled herself about my back, her sharp knees tucked in behind mine, her breasts cold against me, her breath damp between my shoulders, and seemed to fall immediately asleep with a last sigh. And that animal warmth was so intimate that I would not have peeled my skin from hers for all the world. I shall stay awake forever, I thought, I won't waste another moment of her closeness; but then it was morning, and the blind was open and she had detached herself from me in the night and was lying beside me as I found her, marooned on the bed.

Now she is sitting with her knees drawn up on the glinting sunlit white sand, the seals bobbing in the waves, the sea sapphire-blue, as if this were a Riviera — were it not for the cold and the long skirt she has wrapped around her shins against it, and her long boots. The sky clear but for a glairy thickness at the horizon which might be haze or fog or just a trick of the light, a water-sky. The sea is about to turn and has pulled right back, leaving a weedy wet band behind, and comes in flat and sidelong to the shore in unbroken ripples like silk. Further out, a band of darker grey-blue covered in tiny crests, a shelf in the sea-floor perhaps, and beyond that, further still, flat and silver-blue again, some darker striations, out to the earth's curve. Another pale and sun-washed day. It's beautiful, this barren place, in its way.

'Take me north,' she said, and here we are. I had thought it a whim, a nostalgic or romantic wish to return to her wind-swept birthplace, but now we are here I wonder what it is she watches for, if there is some attachment that goes deeper, drawing her back. Is she looking for something she might recognize, out in the waves? A pattern or a colour that speaks of an old home?

She doesn't remember anything. Your house? I ask; the

island?' 'None of it,' she says. 'Only the sea, the sound of the sea, in the night.' These restless waves that wash through her sleep. Like the mermaids' children, I teased, haunted by the sound of the sea in their dreams. Is that it, do you think? Some atavistic affliction, my little half-breed? 'Could be, Professor. Could be my inheritance. For all I know about it,' she said, and I regretted my lack of tact.

She left, she says, when she was too young to remember anything else. There is no trace of an accent, although she says she learned her first words from her father, borrowing his rounded vowels, his consonants, the roll of the tongue like a wave on the shore. Where did he go, I wonder? I find myself unable to ask her, when and why and how could he leave you? He left when she was little; that's all she'll say.

He must have wanted to come back one day, I ventured this morning. She has not, in the past, been forthcoming on the subject.

'Yes, probably,' she said. 'But not with us.'

She stared into her mug, swirled the leaves in the bottom, seeing nothing that she cared to share.

'No,' she said eventually, to herself, still swirling and staring; then abruptly looking up, with a strange and unconvincing smile: 'no, wherever he went, he's long gone.' Then she started washing up, which is not, as far as I have observed in our few weeks of close acquaintance, an activity she is much inclined to. 'I might go out for a bit,' she said when she was finished, wiping her hands on a tea-towel and tossing it on the counter; 'just to get some fresh air. Do you mind?' Of course, I said, of course I don't mind. Evidently I was not invited.

'I'll let you get to work then – the poets await,' she said and, with a kiss, went out.

So I have taken up my station, and she is in her place, looking out. I glance from the window to the page as I work. Her view is encompassed by mine; it is not merely the sea that I see, it is the sea that she is seeing. Something at last takes the empty place at the centre of my perspective. Where I would have been happily confined to my office, deep in the School of English with a view to the red brick wall of the window well, content to grub about in dusty corners, there is now this breadth of vision, this depth and freshness to each breath, this widening space; only her and the horizon. She has brought me the sea and the sky and arranged them around her.

We are quite alone in our little bay. The cottage is an old farmstead built on the flat scrubby links which lead down to a shallow bank, from which it is a short hop to the rocks that slope in turn to the pale sandy shore, bordered with squelchy polypy seaweed and scattered with pebbles, shells, sea-oddments – a scrap of netting, a rubber boot. To the north-east, the land rises rapidly in a series of heightening coves in which hundreds of sea-birds roost, riddled with caves like so many ways into the underworld. Fissures that might widen to swallow her in a torrent.

There is a lighthouse, concealed from our view by the cliffs; at night, we can just see the beam of it swing across the sea. To the west, the black rocks stretch out in a treacherous promontory; the water sprays into crevices, and washes over the flat, square slabs, leaving hundreds of white runnels behind like an offering poured on an altar. Looking out in this direction, the shape of that other uninhabited island hulks in the distance, hazy today in the damp bright air. There are no trees. The islands are a herd of cragged beasts, their scurfy backs just breaking the surface of the water, limbs and bellies and tiny primordial heads far, far beneath; snoozing away the centuries, sleeping their ancient, uninvaded sleep, heedless, while sheep and cattle graze on the tough short crops that grow like moss upon them.

Ours is a snug little lair, built in the low bleak style of these parts, laterally arranged so that the bedroom, kitchen and sitting room each have a large window facing the sea. A paisley-patterned green, cream and red rug on a reddish stone floor that is warm underfoot. There is a comforting clutter of knick-knackery. Framed embroidered samplers and local watercolours of lighthouses on the rough, whitewashed walls. Native seabirds painted on decorative plates and shards of slate; candlesticks and old oil lamps are ranked upon the fireplace; blankets and cushions are piled on the sofa. There is another of these ubiquitous tartans at my back, warming the worn leather of the armchair that I have found so accommodating. Linen lace-edged cloths on the many little tables; there is no want of places to rest a mug or a glass. My notebook, pen, pile of books and fresh cup of tea make an admirably humble still-life on the round table to my side.

I read, and write, and look out to my wife, and to the sea beyond her.

The pale-blue tide is turning, now, roiling and foaming into boiling milk as it comes in. If I shift my reading glasses to the end of my nose I can just make out, from here, the dark torpedo-shaped seals, lifted in the waves, their heads popping out briefly to watch her like cautious periscopes. She sits in her place, beyond the sea's reach, her arms around her legs, quite still, narrow, contained. She could watch the sea for hours, she says. Last night I ran a bath for her, and when she came into the living room, pink and softened, and sat with me by the fire I had ready for her, I took between my fingers the hem of the strange old-fash-ioned cotton nightgown that she favours, and I drew it up and inspected her knees. I inspected very gently, with fingertips and kisses, because I wanted to tease her and this is where she tickles — these two knobbles like a schoolboy's. She wriggled and pressed my hands flat to stop them, so that those two precious kneecaps were cupped wholly in my palms. 'What are you doing?' she laughed. You were out on the beach so long, I said. I'm checking for barnacles.

Her knees cupped in my hands, the cool of the bone, under warm skin.

'Honestly,' she said, laughing. 'Barnacles. Like a grotty old whale.'

Not at all, not at all, I said, sliding my hands over her; it seems you are perfectly smooth. Silken.

And warm, up and over her skin and within.

She stands, looks back, too quick for me to lower my head, push up my glasses and pretend I wasn't looking, peering professorially at her over the rims as if awaiting an answer. She smiles and waves, blithe, bonny girl, pushing her hair from her face, then turns and sets off away from me, along the shoreline, towards the rocks. Later perhaps she will have tales of shells and seals and seaweed to tell. Perhaps she will have found something she was looking for. Perhaps, although she has left me behind, she is thinking of me; perhaps she will bring something back for me.

Yesterday she brought me a gift, a flat black oval from the beach, chosen from the hundreds that scatter the sand, knowing by her weird instinct the one that would perfectly fit my palm. It has dried now to a deep blue-purple like a storm cloud, and next week, when we come to leave here, I will stow it in our luggage and take it home with me and use it as a paperweight, perhaps.

I think of my desk, the battered stained wood buried under all those papers that have strewn my life, ring-stained with the mugs I have used in the absence of this smooth and satisfying piece of stone. How odd, to think of it sitting there in my shut-up office without me. Matthew Stevens has his eye on that desk, I know — it's been there a long time, as long as I have, a lovely old oaken thing that I have stubbornly refused to relinquish through a half-dozen refurbishments, and it is the envy of all the younger cohort who must make do with beech-veneered MDF. I'm coming back, Matthew, I said, catching him stroking a covetous hand as he stood over it. There's no question about that. I have no doubt there was talk, over horrible instant coffee in the common room: 'Surely he'll bow out early, now?' As if I were an old magician in a tattered robe, turning tired tricks to an empty hall. They'll find I have a few more up my sleeve yet. I have committed no sin, no solecism even as far as I'm concerned, and see no reason to feel I must go. I'm sure that I can cope with a few more snickers and whispers at my back.

He blustered, 'But of course you will. I don't know what we'll do without you this term as it is. The place will fall to bits.' Smarmy Professor Stevens, Head of School and fifteen years my junior. 'But you must work on your book. Which I know will be tremendous.' Well, I do what I can, for the sake of our place in the league tables, I said. We must all do our part. I enjoyed your bit in the *Quarterly*, by the way. 'Oh, you read that?' he said casually. There was a copy or two lying around, I said. 'They've picked up a longer piece for the summer, actually,' he said. 'I've a couple of ideas I'm starting to think through . . .' That's splendid, Matthew, I said, splendid. If you'll excuse me, I must just finish clearing up my desk and get home. 'Yes, yes, I expect you *must*,' he said, backing out with a mild leer that I chose not to rise to.

Of course, at that time, she wasn't there to get home to, whatever Stevens was inferring – she only moved in on Friday. I've yet to have the pleasure of finding her there waiting for me. But now, now we are married and she will share my little end-of-terrace – how full the days will be; how satisfying. She has galvanized me. With her at my side, working with me, waiting at home for me, always in my thoughts, I shall produce a work of magnitude. This little anthology of mine might yet soar into a flight of brilliance, weighted to the world with this, her gift to me, this comforting solid stone now couched in the palm of my hand.

Yes, all very well. But will she be content as my amanuensis? I picture us building this legacy together, but those whispers and titters will follow her too. We talked once of her working on her doctorate with me, but that would be impossible now. She hasn't mentioned it, and neither have I. I am putting off the moment when I must part with this part of her, for the sake of what I have gained.

I wonder if I could stand to see her working under someone else. I wonder if I could bear it, in a few years' time, watching her scan her lecture notes over breakfast, waving her off, knowing that a horde of hungry undergrads would soon be slavering over her. And I left at my desk reading fairy-tales. Will I be willing, when the time comes, to give her over to the world?

I turn my flat stone over and over and look out to her there, on the beach, where she

Ah, she has moved again. There she is, walking further off, hands in pockets, head bent; intent, she scours the sand. The seals, too, turn their heads to track her progress, their mournful eyes never leaving her. She seeks, she discards. She selects a shell, perhaps, a pebble, a piece of treasure; inspects it; tosses it to the water, a careless offering.

The distance seems unbroachable, from here to her, the glass between us and the stretch of hard shoal. I know now what it means, to miss someone; for there to be a before and after, a without and a with; to have something to look forward to and so feel the lack in the hours between, the bitter-sweetness of anticipation (I lick my lips and taste marmalade, from her mouth); to feel time passing for the first time in – how long has it been? How much time has slipped from me, neither with nor without? All those years, and suddenly I was sixty and still, after so many untended and unchronicled months, unloved. And not loving. I couldn't say how long it has been since I had something to count the hours for, some reason to differentiate the days. How long I have spent at my papers, thinking myself contented. Or if, indeed, I have ever felt this absence, this need of another being before, in quite this way before. The bodily yearn, of course, but not only that; when I was a smoker, I would sometimes think of lighting a cigarette and realize that I already held a lit one in my hand. As if the craving would always far outreach its satisfaction, as if it was only ever a meagre substitute, an insufficient means of fulfilling a greater and unknown lack. And this is how it is with her; each single instant can never be commensurate to the constant want of her.

But I couldn't give her up.

I'd like a cigarette now. It's been years.

Naturally, I have had lovers. How many? Is there a need to enumerate? Enough. Too many. A sufficiency. More than twenty, less perhaps than thirty. An average then of one every two years, or thereabouts. Such mean numbers being meaningless, naturally – I did not toss about with another toddler in my cot. What a thought. I was, in fact, perhaps predictably a late starter. At eighteen the fat of my lonely, greedy adolescence fell from me and I emerged, lean, hungry, quickened, lusting for learning and love, for brilliant friends and eager bedfellows. I regret that I rarely considered the two to overlap. If ever I catch myself wishing I were forty years younger, I remind myself of this. In truth I'm no better than the doleful clots who followed her at a distance around the campus; I have only eminence on my side. Had I known her then, I wouldn't have known what to do with her. Much as now.

At her age, I had adopted a persona I thought both enigmatic and urbane, and spent my evenings either in the dingy bar of the students' union, talking about girls and poetry over pints of warm weak ale, or else sitting on the narrow beds of said girls, talking about poetry and drinking cheap red wine, quoting Rimbaud and Rilke and smoking slim brown continental cigarettes – yes, my student years were one long unfiltered affectation – running a hand through the poet's mane I'd cultivated, declaiming my own no doubt abysmal verses; all of which would, today, make my wife laugh out loud.

She is out there on the beach this very moment smiling to herself, no doubt. A smile I can't prise open. She has her back to me, but I can tell. Of all those irrelevant women, she is the only one to teach me and to tame me. And I'll be as savage as she wants me, but should she turn her back I'll always be following doggedly behind her, muzzle bowed.

The light is almost faded. Winter is coming, the nights draw in; it is dark as midnight by late afternoon, and cold. She turns to come home; in the dimness I can't make out her features, just the pale of her face. The tide is retreating into itself again, folding back into the clouded horizon, leaving her behind on the shore.

*

She came in chilled from the sea-mist that I felt on my cheek, in turn; she stroked the scrapey shadow that by five comes upon me, grizzled old bear that I am. The smell of the water-soaked air clung to her. A vibration in the dusk about her, a deep-sea coruscation, bright, unseen. She had left her mind looking out, I think. Her eyes were still full of it; slowly, slowly she seemed to see me again, from a depth.

The way she sat this evening: staring into the fire, the glow of her skin, her eyes dark and lively as they followed the flames. She might have been looking into the future, or the past, or through to some other realm entirely. What are you thinking of, I asked. She was silent. I put a hand to her hot cheek; she twisted her mouth to kiss my palm. 'Nothing much,' she said. 'Just fireside thoughts. Bonfires. Chimneys. Chimney-sweeps. Chestnuts. The burning of letters; Shelley's heart in the flames. Shipwreck wood, oak and pine. And so on.' Her voice mesmeric, monotone, as if speaking each flicker as it flared and died, as if listening to the crackle of her own mind kindling. She recited: 'A ruddy shaft our fire must shoot O'er the sea: Do sailors eye the casement – mute, Drenched and stark, From their bark – '

. . . And envy, gnash their teeth for hate O' the warm safe house and happy freight – Thee and me?

She and me. I and she. Safe within, the dark sea outside, and the poor envious sailors who long for home, who cannot have her; the heat of the skin of her chest, her shoulders, as I slid from them shawl and sweater; the small of her back quite cool, the soles of her feet, folded under her, frozen. I clasped my hands about them; the only part of her skin that has toughened, my barefoot urchin.

As I warmed my hands before the grate, the better to administer to her chilled extremities, she unfolded herself and splayed her toes before the fire – yes, they are also just a little webbed, so that each tiny membrane glowed orange, like a frog's foot in the firelight. I pushed my fingers into the gaps and rubbed the knobbles of her big toes with my thumbs. She laughed. 'I hate people touching my feet. My weird feet. Except you. Since you seem to have accepted your frog princess.' No, no, not a frog, I said, wondering if she had been listening to my thoughts as well as her own. I adore your dear, funny feet, I said, kissing them.

Her toenails are still painted red from our wedding – our wedding just a few days ago. A hesitant and shy affair, with her silk-clad at the centre of the hush, so insubstantial that I thought she would vanish with the kiss that sealed it; but no, for all the sniggers and hoots that I imagine my erstwhile colleagues are still enjoying, here she is still, her thin, cool body still in my grasp. My bride, carried off on the north wind, leaving that snide small world behind us.

She sings in the bath. I hear her, splashing happily in her own safe little sea and humming.

We have been telling each other the tale of our great romance, as I suppose all newlyweds do; refining the details, spinning it out, combing and weaving the threads of it. I insist, and will persist in doing so, however inconceivable it may seem: she chose me. She turned her obfuscate eyes upon me and enthralled me for ever. In a corner of the seminar room, listening quietly, it was she who first smiled, as if we shared a secret joke. It was she who laid a hand upon my arm, as if careless of her gestures. It was she who sought me out.

We met, I told her, that September afternoon; one by one you all shuffled into that dingy basement room and took your seats; remember? The scratched wood, the smell of stale instant coffee and radiators and books, a library damped and then dried in the central heating many times over; the old ribbed brown carpets, the dust. The familiar new-term feeling. She entered last, a tall impossible girl with bright silver hair hanging in tangles to her waist. We watched her, the other students and I, as she took her seat haughtily in the corner. She didn't speak. When I checked their names, she only nodded, raised her eyes and nodded, and for a moment I faltered, even then.

You came in last, I told her, and you took your seat far away from me, in a corner. You brought the cold in with you, the crisp of the first frost and the leaves already falling; they were tangled in your hair – 'They were not,' she said, with a little shove, 'I'm not a vagrant' – but so I saw you, darling, an autumn sprite, come in from the first chill. You wore a purple sweater, the colour of the heather on the heath . . .

'Heather blooms in spring,' she said. 'And I have never owned a purple sweater.' As if you'd just come down from a hilltop, I insisted, as if you'd just conjured yourself out of the north wind, dressed in heather, and your eyes all clouded . . . 'It was green. I've never had a purple one. I've had it for years, it's one of my favourites. I remember wearing it. Sometimes I think I could remember what I wore every Tuesday of that term, because I always chose carefully. For your seminar. For you.' I was touched, and I confess a little surprised; she seems quite without regard for her apparel, seems to cover her nakedness in whatever misshapen garment comes to hand; but also, I was bewildered. How could she scratch out, so easily, this image of her I had so treasured and thought indelible? How, after a year of existing in that guise in my mind, how can she possibly say: I have never been thus; I have never owned, much less worn, a purple sweater?

'You don't like it in green?' she asked. 'I don't wear purple. I never do. I wear green. And grey. I hadn't realized you'd married me for sartorial reasons,' she said. 'If that's the case, well . . .' and her naked shoulders rose within her tartan toga, 'sorry about that.'

No, no, it's not that, you are beautiful whatever you wear, I said, but the heather, the heather all about you and the north wind and the warm wool drawn about your neck . . . 'Yes, yes,' she said. 'With leaves in my hair and a cobweb for a shawl and so forth. All ready to cast my spell on you.'

So she arrived in my seminar room, and so began the chaste months of our unspoken courtship. Yes, chaste; there were no sordid trysts in my office, no indecorous desk-top wrangling. What followed was rather a tormented year of glances; chance meetings in corridors or the common room, where I had never previously deigned to venture, and yet now found myself frequently passing through, hoping to find her reading there: long legs folded up under her, her shoes discarded, her rough heel encircled by a balded patch of sock so that I longed to poke it with a finger. Ten or fifteen times a day I'd drift down the stairs, pausing on the landing to survey the sofas, a hopeless ghost, and she was more often absent than not. Sometimes a week would go by without her, and sometimes it was all I could do not to go to her usual perch in the bay window, to seek out some last warm hint of scent; and sometimes that was more than I could do, and I'd idle over, take up some journal or paper from the table, lean casually with a hand on the place she might lately have been curled. And if I found that precious trace there then the comfort of it could barely compensate the ache of her recent departure, of coincidence just missed, or the possibility that it wasn't her warmth at all.

But there were times when she was there, and times when she would look up from her book and smile, and cup her heel in her palm and blush. I would hover over her, do my best to string out a passing comment about her last essay, or a book I thought she'd find interesting or useful, or the weather, God help me . . . What were her holiday plans, was she looking forward to Christmas, to Easter? And she'd shrug, not impolitely, and stare unblinking up at me as I foundered and flailed like a schoolboy. In seminars, she kept her chin lowered, blushing quickly when I caught her looking; in lectures, she was not so coy. I watched her hand curl over the page while her strange eyes never left me, as if she was entranced, and I found myself performing for her, embellishing, all the old stories invigorated – without quite admitting the reason, I found a new energy for material I'd thought long worn thin by repetition. She laughed at my quips, she lingered after classes to clarify a point, but never long enough to leave us quite alone together. Sometimes as I left for home and locked up my office I would think I'd seen a flick of silver, disappearing around the corner of the corridor.

As the summer term drew to a close, she came to see me of her own accord. A knock and there she was, twisting her hair in the doorway. She wanted to talk about postgraduate study, or that is what she said, and I had no reason at the time to doubt it. It was natural that she should ask me to supervise her work, an obvious fit of research interests, nothing more. Preposterous to hope for an ulterior motive, I thought, or rather didn't allow myself to think. We spent an hour in my stuffy office, I in a pose of pretended ease, swivelling gently on my chair, she perched on my baggy sofa with her bare knees bent level with her chest. She rubbed a hand down her sharp bare shinbone, she twisted her hair and ruffled it at the back and lifted it from her neck. All this, and the promise of a further year or more of her made my scalp throb in a way I was still ignoring. As she talked through her ideas, she was more animated than I'd ever seen her; ambitious, articulate, and something crackling behind her eyes, distracting me from her bare skin, her long shins, the hair stuck to her neck. It was not only all that; I didn't only want her, although by then I could hardly deny I did; I also wanted, very much, to work with her, to catch the spark of her. I urged her to apply. She said she was still thinking about it, she'd need to look into funding, or something similar, something non-committal, and shrugged and seemed extinguished. If there's anything I can do, I said, emphatically, and meant it. I would have done, would do, anything. I walked her to the door and took the tiny, scintillating liberty of putting a hand on her shoulder. She thanked me, suddenly shy again and rather formal, and I told her, 'Call me Richard.' She only smiled. Blushed, perhaps; perhaps not. It was hot.

She says it with a hesitancy that delights me, after so many years of being only 'Professor _____', that name now also her own. I seem somehow to have always fallen in to that division of the faculty known by their proper titles, even before these venerable last years of seniority; the younger lecturers, with their haircuts and jeans and open shirts with affected, Bohemian cravats (Dr Evans, that ass), were 'Matthew' or 'Mark' or even 'Felicity', but no one ever ventured a 'Richard'. I have always been Professor _____, Prof to the cocky ones. And now I am her Richard, and how I love to hear her say my name.

A strand of scented steam has crept from under the bathroom door and through the cottage so that the air smells of her skin, biscuity salt and sweet underlying the woodsmoke and the draughts of sea-air that can never be quite excluded. I am left alone now, surrounded by our discarded garments, and have pulled a blanket about me and can hear her splashing.

Yes, it is such a pleasure to dwell on the tale alone, while she is in her bath, and not here to interject with her nonsense about not wearing purple.

I opened my house for her, on the last afternoon of the summer term. Such depths of subterfuge I sunk to; I invited the whole lot of them, my graduating class, to a late buffet lunch, just for her sake, just to see her one more time. And I fretted for a week beforehand like the old fusspot I am, losing sleep over how to marinate the chicken, and where to buy my cheeses, and did she like olives (and would she come?), could she eat nuts (would she come?), did she drink red or white or both or neither (would she come, would she come, when she'd said she would come?). I'd a fine dessert wine imported from Spain, it was heady, clover-scented stuff; we'd drink it with strawberries on the lawn, if she would only stay long enough to let them stain her lips . . . these, and others like them, were the thoughts that beset me every night for a week, until dawn. I was up at the crack of it, that morning; I cleaned and tidied so aggressively that the place looked unloved, unlived-in. I messed it up again a little, scattering a few books and papers. There was little else to create the illusion of contented clutter.

But in the light of that exhausted morning, with the clarity of vision that comes with sleeplessness or fever, I saw how shabby it all was: my one sagging armchair the only comfortable seat in the room; the cushions too stiff, small and formal, and not quite matching the sofa. I tried pulling across the nets that hung behind the old blue drapes, but that only made things worse – they wouldn't quite meet, and trapped the sunshine in a single shaft of terrible light, all the dust, all my flakey skin-scurf hanging suspended in it, illuminating with that single beam the truth, that this was unmistakably the burrow of a bachelor, a fading, thinning old man. But no. I am, as she says, only sixty, and have a full head of hair. Run a hand through it to be sure, Richard.

I pulled the drapes back and told myself that in the late afternoon, in the evening, the light would be kinder, a wine-softened, end-of-term light. And this, with the French doors thrown wide to the garden which, despite or because of a want of attention, was luxuriant, created I hoped just the right impression, a shambolic and mature and cosy setting for the evening's host, the wise, welcoming Professor. And they all came, and the light was indeed gentle and the wine well chosen and the mood deferent, and I started to think I should have made this a tradition long ago after all – I started to enjoy it, revelling in their esteem.

She was the last to arrive, or so I recall; possibly there were others, after, rendered irrelevant by her arrival. The agony of waiting and the heart-stopping doorbell announced an endless stream of chumps and braggarts, nonchalant bigheads and idiots, and I did the rounds with Pimm's and lemonade to start, with a kick of good gin. And at last, when it seemed my humble sitting room and its little garden couldn't possibly accommodate one more pair of broad rower's shoulders, or even one more of the alternative, skinny long-lanky variety, at last she arrived. She took me by surprise, I was mid-debate with some clod with an opinion, she'd rang and no one answered so she'd come round the back, she said, finding the gate open, and materialising there in my garden from behind the roses, Queen Rose of the rosebud garden of girls . . . Come in, I said, come into the garden; the brief night goes by in babble and revel and wine, I recited wryly, or pompously or hysterically possibly, reeling. She had brought a bottle, sweet girl. A surprisingly good white Bordeaux.

She confessed to me, later, that she knew nothing about wine and had wanted to impress me; she had entrusted her eight pounds to the helpful chap in Oddbins and he'd chosen, I suppose, a fail-safe; yet how she smiled with a knowing grace when I thanked her, how she dissembled good taste!

I brought out my fine sweet wine and the strawberries, dropping one in each glass as I poured, and I could see no way to circuit and end at her side and so had to pass her, and move on with a wrench to the next. And then found a vantage point from which, while I nodded and thoughtfully frowned and guffawed on cue, I could watch her. I trembled, I had to set my glass down between mouthfuls, I realized I was drunk, now, drunk with the glow of her skin and her bright hair in the low light and with wine. I watched as she sipped and chatted, chatted and sipped, and every time that nectar touched her lips it brought a little private smile to them, a honeyed intoxicated smile, and a flush spreading, and as I saw her drain her glass I rushed to her side to refill it, or attempted to rush, halted as I was by a hundred frustrations – pleasantries, platitudes, gratitudes and top-ups – and as I drew closer I saw her dip her two fingers into her glass to fish for the strawberry at the bottom, wine-soaked, and succeed at last in retrieving it just as I reached her side, so that – delicious! – she turned to see me just as it met her lips, and blushed that most becoming strawberry-red, and said, 'I love this wine! And your house, and your garden . . . This is so nice of you, such a nice way to end the term – Richard.'

And now she is calling me from the bathroom: 'Richard!'

I love to hear her call my name.

Tuesday

We had a visit, this morning, from our Mrs Odie. She'd brought eggs with her; she peered around my bulk and spied my wife skulking shyly behind me. 'A guid braykfast, yir lassie needs,' she said; 'hid's a muggry day the day.' Or something to that effect. I took six and flashed her my most wolfish smile.

Mrs Odie it seems will drop by now and again to 'do for us', as I believe they used to say, although perhaps not here, but in more decorous places; this morning she swept and dusted around us, and made the bed (which we had left rumpled and faintly damp), and washed the dishes in the sink disapprovingly. In fact, she emanated disapproval throughout her interminable visit, during which my wife remained serene and silent like a dozing cat curled on the sofa, while I hovered anxiously and always, seemingly, in precisely the spot that required sweeping, dusting, or otherwise bringing to rights.

I am, on the whole, a man well-liked by strangers. By lovers, colleagues, acquaintances, less so. I believe my wife is the only one who loves me. But in the lecture theatre, the seminar room, the conference hall, I know how to impress. I have held audiences rapt, weaving stories and teasing them out again while they look on, as if gathered about a fire in the darkness. I am of a type: literary, stentorian; steely, black-browed, broad; a deep-set eye with a glint perhaps of mischief – and this has in the past served me well, with students, with strangers. Alas, it seems my wiles and charms are quite toothless when put to work upon the unassailable Mrs Odie. I cannot tell if it is we who disgust her, our way of life – mine, that is; the girl is surely blameless, a captive victim – or if it is life in general, the process of living, the persistent dirtying and sweating and shedding of skin and crumbs and sand, the helpless traces we leave behind us.

When she'd gone, at last, with a farewell frown at my growling stomach – again, I tried to compensate with a grin – I scrambled the eggs and piled them on toast and placed them on the table before my wife. She scraped them off the toast, so that she could pull the bread apart with her fingers before shovelling the eggs back onto each torn fragment with a fork held in her right hand. She eats intently, with a concentration that makes dining with her, more often than not, a sedulous, concise, and largely silent affair. I find watching even this compelling. The last morsel gone, she brushed her fingertips together and smiled at me and said, 'Yum. What a nice woman.' In what way, in what way do you think so? 'Well, I don't know. But eggs are nice for breakfast.' I must remember, I thought, to always have eggs at the ready, and to always plate them on the side of her toast.

She roused me early this morning by hoisting the blind, a ritual that evidently I have previously slept through, unaware of her rising and standing there, unaware of the new space beside me. This time, however, I woke, to a stream of mote-bright early light falling upon her empty white pillow, Zeus seeking out his Danae and finding only an aging don, clutching the bedding to my pale and sparse-furred pectorals. She was at the window, gazing out at the gloaming, or its opposite; whatever the dawn word is for that purple dusk – I would like to say gladdening. And it was, to see her, pale nymph in her nightgown, and a band of turquoise across the horizon, and the maiden moon fading at the sun's approach, creeping behind the thickening clouds. But she was hugging herself, her shoulder blades sharp under the cloth, and when I said her name I saw her take a long breath in and let it out and shudder a little as if shaking something off before coming back to bed, and resting her cheek on my chest, wetly. 'I was dreaming again. I dreamt of a wave,' she said quietly, apologetic. 'The water coming for me. I was backed up against the rock, against a cliff, pinned there, I couldn't move and the water was coming, licking at me like a creature, wrapping itself round my legs, winding up me, and then I was pulled from the rock, something pulled me in, and under, and out, and I couldn't . . . I let it take me, I couldn't fight.'

Should I have acceded to her wish, to bring her to this sea that so disturbs her sleep – and mine? My poor Andromeda. You haven't slept properly since we got here, I said. 'I know. It's exhausting,' she said.

The sea, this morning, does indeed have a gathering look, as if something swells and darkens beneath the flat, wind-flecked surface, which surges and sheens like a leathery hide. I feel I should keep watch, in case the beast should heave out of the water to claim her, but there is no sign of any Kraken broaching the surface, and I believe we are safe for the time being. The sky, however, is bulking out, bloated purple, tumorous. Out on the sand, my wife seems untroubled by the fine, constant drizzle in the air – a 'driv', says Mrs Odie – heavier than mist but not quite falling, it being, as mentioned, a 'muggry' day. My vocabulary is expanding with words I would prefer to have no use for.

She's pulled her hands inside her coat sleeves, curled up and hibernating damply in their burrows. Despite the weather, she does not give up her vigil. Waiting for a sail, perhaps, a sign. I declined to join her out in the driv. I certainly have no inclination to abandon my cosy tartan vantage point. But I must go shopping; she seems happy enough in her own company, and it is my turn to cook.

At her suggestion, we will take it in turns to prepare our evening meals. I have tried to insist that she mustn't trouble herself. I have been entertained by her before, if that is the word for it, and have sampled already the fruits of her labours. She has a gift for the contrary, for transforming innate qualities into their opposites: crisp leaves turn to mulch, the most tender meat toughens, what might be moist stales in her keeping to become heavy and dry; even tinned custard, in her custody, somehow becomes lumpen. Rock cakes you could build walls with; eggs scrambled to a single, solid wad of brown rubber. Once, she made a chicken pie that made me want to weep; I had never thought to taste its like again. Thick lardy pastry, still grey and raw at the centre; white fat on the bacon; stringy greyish meat dissolving into a sauce bound by long strands of watery burnt onion; she might have learned to cook in my school kitchen. I was transported, I was thirteen years old again and consumed by the familiar savourless taste of boredom and hunger and fattishness; one evening after another tasting of that same brown seep of onion; that cold, furtive dorm room, every night always just a little too chilly, and too long. Poor, portly Richard, gobful of sadness and gloopy chicken pie. I finished the plateful in an orgy of masochistic nostalgia, and fear that now she will consider it a favourite.

Last night she attempted sausages. Each fat finger both blackened and bloody, thrust like a swollen fist into an impossible mountain of pale grey mash I couldn't hope to conquer, awash with bilgy gravy; and of course, as always, too much salt; as if the air here were not already laden with it, as if it weren't already crusting every crevice and crack. I took a cautious mouthful, squeezing a smile between my bulging cheeks, sparing myself, for a moment, the gluey ordeal of swallowing, while she watched hopefully. I slathered on mustard. She watched as I hacked up and choked down two of my four sausages, each chunk dutifully ploughed into the pasty potato, which showed no sign of diminishing in quantity. Eat, I said, it will get cold, although it had arrived on the table barely tepid to begin with; did I want her to share my tribulation? Pay penance for inflicting this last indignity upon a poor defenceless pig? She edged her knife tentatively into the stodgy pile on her own plate, and pulled it clean between her lips — somehow I have never minded these dreadful manners of hers. She looked for a moment almost stricken, almost shocked, and reddened and said, 'Oh, I'm sorry. It's awful, isn't it.' I closed my hand over the back of hers, which was still holding the knife she'd licked. I tried to think of something reassuring, and said yes, I'm afraid so. You have excelled yourself. She bit her lip, shamefaced, and I couldn't help laughing. 'Don't,' she said ruefully, 'it really is vile.' Yes. Putrid. She smiled a little. 'Turgid,' she concurred. Rancid. 'Obnoxious.' Stomach-churning. 'Emetic!' she cried, laughing at last. And we abandoned our plates and retired to the sitting room, with bread and cheese, and wine and stories.

The first time I took her to dinner, she ate lobster. She pulled it apart with her hands and licked my fingers.

I took her to a favourite bistro of mine, to which I'd always longed to bring a lover. A romantic spot in its old-fashioned way, I'd found it tucked away down a narrow lane fifteen years before and somehow never thought anyone quite suitable to join me at my lone table by the window. It had been my little treat, to take myself out for a solo supper upon finding the cupboard bare on a weekday evening; a book, a bottle, the satisfaction of public solitude, of looking the part. But here, at last, was my opportunity to play the suitor. How carefully casual the invitation had been – the library was closing, and since we were in town, perhaps we'd have a bite at a little place I knew . . . ? And now it seemed ridiculous, the white cloth on the table and a red rose between us, sitting opposite this extraordinary girl I couldn't possibly have a right to, wondering if I was making a fool of myself, if I had misunderstood her entirely. We'd barely touched, then; we had not transgressed any boundary. A brush of a kiss in greeting, a hand on an arm. This was only perhaps a month ago, as the cautious summer drew to a close. It seems now a long-distant agony, it seems unimaginable, that uncertainty, like recalling an affliction when one is well again, and one cannot remember the moment it was over, the last ebb of sickness or pain.

Am I now so very sure of her? I think so. I turn the stone in my hand, and look for her form on the saturated beach; it takes me a moment to find her, a smear on the glass, but still, there she stands, staring out.

The headwaiter, a consummate professional, came to attend on us personally. He drew her chair out for her, elegantly masked the inevitable double-take when she turned her face to thank him; snapped the crisp white napkin out and let it float down upon her lap like settling snow, and over her head, caught my eye and signalled with the subtlest moue his pleasure – the professor at last did not dine alone. I fear I blushed.

I ordered steak – 'your usual, *monsieur*? *L'entrecote, bleu?*' said the maître d', whom I have never believed is French. She pulled bread from the crust, spreading crumbs over the menu that was pinned under her elbows, surveying it behind the curtain of her hair with head bowed; looked up, looked lost, shrugged sweetly. He suggested, of course, that she try *l'homard*. I, feeling magnanimous, feeling manly, urged her to do so. It was set before her bright-boiled red and butter-gleaming, a beast of a thing, but she set to undaunted with pliers and prongs, shell cracking in her strong hands, and she sucked the meat from its pincers, and even offered me an appendage from her fingers before licking them clean, shamelessly, grinning. She is doing her best to learn, she has told me, how to eat in 'fancy places'. To set down her knife and fork, and take a sip of wine, and make conversation. She wasn't raised that way, she says. She remains evasive on the details of which way she was. But I could happily have sat in silence and watched as she devoured one chunk and claw after another, until the plate was cleared and the broken, empty carcass piled into the bowl beside her. She's said since that she was nervous, but seemed at ease; although I do remember now that she drank half a glass of wine in one draught. I remember watching as the colour came into her cheeks, as red as the rose between us, as if she had been in need of a transfusion. Her eyes gleaming silver.

How I relished the studious not-staring of the other diners as she put her hand on mine and blushed deeper! She did not wither or fade under scrutiny. She twisted at my fingers almost distractedly, like a curious child, twisting and twisting in that way she has, in that way I now know she has; but this was the first time she twisted, my guts knotting about her knuckles, twisting a rope down to the root of my groin until I could bear it no longer and grasped her fingers tightly, squeezing them still in my fist. And then, and then, she pulled my hand towards her and kissed the end of my index finger and then – extraordinary girl! – took the tip into her mouth and sucked it for a second, just as she had sucked the butter from her own, her lips still oily with it, her virgin lips. And then drew back, smiling, blushing, my hand trembling where she'd left it suspended and faintly glistening, and she said, 'It's rude to point, my mother told me.' Your mother! I said, struggling to keep my voice even and pull myself together. And what would your mother say if she could see you here with me, with your erudite but undeniably aging mentor, sucking on his learned fingers?

A little frown occluded her eyes then; but she dispelled it just as quickly and said, 'I'd imagine she'd tell you it's rude to point,' folding away my finger, 'and besides, you're only sixty.'

Only sixty, she said. Still vigorous, still lusty. Tall and trim. Yet in latter years I have noticed, though I don't care to admit it, how quickly I grow weary when I exert myself; and these last few days and nights, I have found that certain activities call for far greater exertion than they once did.

Last night I lay in bed waiting for her, listening to her in the bathroom, peeing quietly with the tap running, scrubbing her face, cleaning her teeth. She crept into the room, drew back the blankets – we sleep under three heavy, scratchy woollen tartans – exposing me head to foot to the lamplight, and lifted her nightgown to her hips and clambered aboard, at once shameless and utterly coy; and rocked herself upon me, as patient and steady as the wash of waves on the shore, watching intently, and the surge of the tide grew stronger until I gripped her hips and she cried out silently, a moment of arrest that seemed unending.

At last she took one huge breath and let it out shakily and clambered off again, pulling her gown back down to her ankles and the blankets up over both of us and sighing softly beside me, leaving me awed, spent, my heartbeat alarming, slowing slowly to the rhythm of the ocean.

She falls asleep instantly; these few nights I have spent with her, she has swum deep before I have even steadied my breath. And as she dreams her submarine dreams I lie beside her, a whale's carcass, a wrecked ship, a vast ribcage in the dark blue deep; and she is a tiny luminescent silver fish, picking me clean, in and out of all that's left of me, bare bones long since freed of flesh or rigging.

Our wedding night, four nights ago: the brittle excitement of the afternoon quieting as we came into my bedroom and I closed the door behind us. I had made up the bed with new white sheets, still creased and smelling of the plastic packing; it seemed wrong to lay her down on old bedding when she was herself unused. I turned on the bedside lamp, closed the curtains, while she stood in the middle of the room, watching me, not moving. I could see her breathing. As I moved towards her, unsure how to approach, she slipped from her white silk as if it were another skin, to reveal the white silk of her own; pale pink areolae, green veins coursing just below the surface; her long spine, a kiss for each bone-tip; a violet mole like a fishtail by her hip-bone, an arrowhead pointing to the fine-spun untamed bright white floss of her pubis. She put her arms about my neck and swung her legs about my waist and clung there, little limpet; her anxious eagerness, a gasp, biting her lip, biting my skin and clinging . . .

Enough, enough. I must let her alone, and go out.

*

The island has a shop, fifteen minutes' walk from our cottage, cutting across the narrow middle to a long, wide bay on the south-west side, where the town, such as it is, clusters. The town consists of a hotel, a fishery, a crafts centre, a squat pebble-dashed new church replacing the old one ruined on the hill, and yes, a shop, singular – and singular indeed it is. An unassuming exterior, a low stone building not unlike our little cottage; the red door, which announces customers with a bright ting of a bell, gives way to a cavern of delights, every corner crammed full; shelves from floor to ceiling, a central bench piled with some rather sorry-looking fresh produce and a mound of turnips, a refrigerated wall at the back stacked with packaged meat and fish, milk, cheese, cans and bottles; bins and buckets full of plastic spades, seashells, umbrellas and optimistic paper parasols . . . I bought a new notebook; I bought two steaks, a haggis and the smallest turnip I could find; a big crab caught off the shore of this island and already picked; Hellmann's mayonnaise, a weighty chewy loaf, salad leaves of a sort, salted peanuts; several bottles, including a dubious, dusty Chianti and a superlative single malt to replenish my flask. Yes, I shop like a bachelor, still. I bought a newspaper – yesterday's *Times* the best on offer – and a book of folklore, tales of the trows and faeries and witches and mermaids that it is not hard to imagine still haunt these islands; the book had a stand of its own and was the work, I gathered, of a local author. I thought this purchase a gracious gesture, wishing for some reason to please Mr Begg behind the counter. I'm working on folktales, fairy-tales, myself, I said to him. 'Oh, aye?' he said, without betraying any interest or curiosity. In the nineteenth century, I explained. 'Aye,' he nodded. Have you read this one? I asked. 'Aye,' he answered, a little more warmly perhaps, some enthusiasm kindling in his little marbley eyes, buried deep from years of being screwed against the wind. 'It's no bad.' He took my turnip to the scale to weigh it. It appeared the conversation was over.

There are two rows of big glass jars behind the counter. For the sake of nostalgia, I asked for a bag of aniseed balls. God knows how long these little cochineal orbs have been rattling around there; how sad that those jars of jewels lose their dazzle when one is old and rich enough to fill sacks full, how sad that the child with only tenpence will never fulfil that dream, which will have tarnished by the time he can attain it. If, indeed, there are any children here; it could be that they've all long since grown old, on this aging island. I watched him fetch down the jar, weigh them with a timeless clatter on the metal scale, pour them into their little paper bag and pinch it closed with neat, thick fingers the colour of uncooked veal; unmistakably a Scotsman's hands, with red-blond hairs at wrist and knuckle.

I might also have bought a hoe, a screwdriver, a mallet; sticking plasters, painkillers, tampons, nappies; fuse wire, a sewing kit, a tape measure, scissors, batteries, decorative painted rocks . . . I doubt I could think of a thing I needed, or would never need, that was not hidden away in there. I might also have bought a waterproof poncho from the small pile helpfully, hintingly displayed by the till, but regrettably, did not.

I left with a nod and an inscrutable smirk from Mr Begg. (I believe he thought I'd bought the sweeties, as he called them, for my 'peedie lass' – he asked after her. She has not to my knowledge set foot in the shop since our arrival. I suppose she has been seen on the beach. News, unlike newspapers, travels fast here it seems.) I emerged under a blackening sky, the air already condensing into sheer water; as I came over the ridge to descend to our side of the island, I saw a cloud over the sea blood-purple like an omen, staining the water black, and spreading through it to the shore as if the Kraken had been slaughtered in my absence; the island to the west of ours had vanished in the air. I could not see her on the beach. Within ten yards the heavens, if such they are in these parts, had opened above me and there was barely a gap of air to breathe in through the downpour. I began to run, awkwardly, the bags heavy, wine clanking, the turnip bashing against my knee like a primitive football; I held both bags in one hand so that I could cover my head with my precious newspaper, and jogged home at a painful, limping gait, arriving soaked through, gulping for breath, my right shoulder and forearm and bicep on fire, one palm throbbing and tingling as the blood returned to the swollen white ridges left behind by the plastic handles, and the other stained by a handful of useless, inky pulp. I shook out the pages, the letters running irretrievably, I swiped the water from my wax-jacket sleeves, I ruffled and shook my hair like a drenched dog. I called for her, my shout drowned by the rain on the roof, on the windows, the little house assailed from every possible angle; I looked into the bedroom, the kitchen as I passed, calling, calling, until I came back to the sitting room, and automatically looked for her out on the beach, but there wasn't a trace of her left on the wet sand, and I wondered for a moment if she'd been washed away after all before seeing her damp head peep around the back of my chair, a thick wet cord of hair hanging; she was so balled up that no other part of her protruded.

'You're back!' she said, 'Did you get caught in the rain?' Yes, I said. Yes, I evidently did. I called for you, you didn't answer . . . 'It's wild out there!' she said, ignoring me, and her eyes, too, were wild for a moment, her fingers gripping the wing of the chair, peering round the back of it like a goblin. In the dim light she seemed somehow unearthly, touched with the hysteria of the wind, and I wondered how long she had stood out there, soaking to the skin; but then she said, perfectly calmly, 'I'll make some tea, would you like some?' as if she were nothing more than my ordinary young wife. Yes, I would, I said; yes, please. Wait, I'll make it.

One dark November day a year ago, she came into my seminar room drenched with the rain, and while the other students shook out their umbrellas and pulled off sodden hats and coats, she just took her seat, her clothes clinging as if she'd just walked out of the ocean, her hair long and waterlogged and droplets running down the ropes of it, and dripped on her desk. She seemed on the point of dissolution, as if the whole of her was pouring away, and yet quite unaware. She sneezed, once, and sniffed throughout the session. You'll catch your death, I nearly said, and felt compelled even then to fold her into my coat, to take her home and unpeel her and wrap her in blankets, but didn't. One of the other girls whispered something to her friend, and they sniggered, and I could have torn their throats out.

She has no memory of this day. I'm not sure she noticed the rain, at the time, at all.

She brought a towel from the bathroom, rubbing at her head and then mine, and sat by my feet and we sipped our tea and watched the sky changing, watched the rain slacken; and I could not stop myself asking, Why did we come to this grey place? 'Are you sad, Richard?' she said. 'It's not just grey.' And pointing out to where the sea met the sky, which seemed for now to have slaked itself, her eyes following her own finger as it traced the fine gradations up to the apex, or the limits of the window frame: 'See? Silver. Pewter. Old bronze. Oyster shell.' Graphite, dove's wing, goosedown, I said. 'Lead.' Cigar smoke. 'Ash.' Sere. Slate. Cinereal. This especially pleased her. And on we went, this favourite diversion that already seems part of a half-forgotten past, like an old couple playing an old game; on we went naming the grey until it seemed that a rainbow spectrum was a common, gaudy and frivolous thing next to this muted subtlety of shades.

And then all at once, a crack appeared in the cloud, the sun at one corner of it like a god's eye, casting a piercing lancet across the sky; and then one after another, rods of silver broke through to announce his presence. Like some awful ruthless salvation, the sun burned the edge of the cloud-bank magnesium white, and shone brilliant on the still-tender, cleansed world; the rock pools transformed into blinding mirrors and the sea, so lately needled to fury, was lulled and banded with whispering silver as it approached the shore, and there was the terrible argent fire of the cloud's lining after the storm; and . . . 'Let's go out!' she said. 'In the sunshine . . .' As if extinction had not threatened only an hour before. 'Let's explore,' she said. And I was so glad to be asked, to be required, that I couldn't refuse her, so we put on sweaters and hats and stepped out, both still a little damp within our clothes, a little shivery, emerging into the rawness of the new world and the air stripped clean. She put an arm through mine, cosily, and sighed. 'I'm glad we came here,' she said. 'Thank you for seeing me safe over the sea.'

Climbing up from the beach, we took the little path that leads up to the old kirk, on its lonely mound overlooking the bay. Sunk in the centre of the churchyard, the old grey mossy chapel. Broken steps led down to the deep rectangle of the paved floor. A hollow place, the sanctuary quiet sheared by the cries of the gulls and the hush of the ocean. Through the empty, glassless arch of the window, the sea paling into the horizon, and a glimpse of the little harbour on the other side of the bay. Standing looking up through the long-fallen roof, the nerves in my neck pressed, I felt dizzied by the scutter and race of the clouds, the sky washed thin, pressure lifted too high. Birds spiralling, shredding the silence after the squall, screaming. I looked down and reached for her blindly, blood flowing back up to my eyes in a dark whirlpool; I found her hand, thin, cold, and remembered clasping it when we were married, so few days ago, an age ago. How cold it was in that sparse office with its meagre flowers on the desk, white spray and pink roses browning at the edges; her own bouquet, three white calla lilies I had picked out for her, she clutched to her chest. The registrar looking from one to the other as if it were a practical joke, expecting the groom to arrive at any moment and take her off my hands. I'm not here to give her away, if that's what you're thinking, I said. Nothing could persuade me to do that. He smiled, polite, professional, turned the book for us to sign. I took it upon myself to kiss my bride.

And now here we were in a church, unfit for a ceremony, without guests, without priests, without gowns and roses and lilies, but still, here was the solemnity we'd missed; still I took her cold hand and asked again if she would take this man, if she would promise me again to be my wife. There before the broken old stone altar; there under the wind-blown gulls; there within sight of the sea, I asked if she would still have me. And she said yes. She didn't laugh at me or evade my eyes. She just said, 'Yes'. And held my hands for a long time.

As we reached the cemetery gate, we passed a woolly huddle of an old man, crouching by a weathered stone; he cannot possibly have been grieving, as old as he was, at that ancient grave, the occupant centuries dead. He raised his eyes as we passed, watching her go. Our only witness.

On the path back she found a little lower jawbone, belonging, I think, to some hapless rabbit. The bottom tooth jutting, wobbly in its gumless hole. She has strung a ribbon through it, and hung it from her neck. You grow stranger every day, I'm sure, I said. 'Ah, you hardly know me yet,' she said. My strange wife, arranging her talismans about her. You don't wear jewellery, I said. 'It's hardly jewellery. It's not exactly diamonds,' she scoffed. No, I said. Quite right. There it hangs alongside the rings I gave her in troth, tiny, fragile and sharp, just below her collar bone, which is also fragile and sharp.

The sea quiet, calm, ungrasping, and the air clear; light twinkling on the water, the breaking glimmering surface, cohering at the horizon into a sheen of pale gold. Beside me, she shone, as if filled with it, the light from the sea numinous, a grace to meet her own. We watched the light scintillate until it dimmed, until only a sparkle or two remained, as if signalling, until darkness had fully fallen. It does fall, here, it falls softly, in a blanket of night-colours, deep brown and green and viscous blue; nothing like the false, city-stained night we are accustomed to, held at bay by streetlights. It has settled all about the house, softly.

Tonight she laid me down, my head upon her outstretched legs, supine, and I balanced a glass of whisky on my belly while she stroked at my temples, where the lighter grey meets the black, where I am almost distinguished. All through the evening I spooled out stories for her, going back over my gatherings of the day. I told tales of island sorcery. The Sirens, Sycorax; Circe and the pigs she made of men. She snorted in recognition.

I don't question, I don't want to know about the swine that have snuffled around her. It doesn't matter to me; I do not know or wish to know of those she has, in the past, enchanted, those shambling lovelorn louts that circled her from a wistful distance. I know enough. I know, because she's told me, and because I found it for myself just four nights ago: she was waiting, all that time. Waiting for her one true love, she says, sweetly, sing-song – there is none like her, none. At twenty-one, still patient, still waiting. And yet so eager, and yet so shy; her instinct, unpractised, guiding her hand. My Lamia, a virgin purest lipped, and yet of love deep learned to the red heart's core.

I told of Vivien, or Nimue or Niviane; the huntress, the sometime Lady of the Lake . . . I grew expansive, settling into the old routine, gesturing in the air above me as if casting grandiloquent spells, and she stroked, stroked at my temples, and it was I who was spellbound.

'I know Vivien,' she said, 'I know this one.' Oh yes? I said. 'Yes, you've told me this before.' Am I beginning to repeat myself? I wondered. When? 'Oh, you couldn't have known. It was before you met me.' She bent her head, whispered, 'I followed, but you marked me not.' What are you talking about? I asked, thoroughly confused; she seemed to be enjoying herself. She laughed. 'Why don't *I* tell *you* our story, from the beginning this time,' she said. 'It was summer. I was warm, so I was wearing, I imagine, a T-shirt. Let's say it was grey. Or green. I sat at the back.' When, when, what can you mean? I asked. 'Your lectures. I came to all of your lectures, in my second year, in the summer term. The first was Tennyson, it was the *Idylls of the King*. Merlin.' And, of course, his Vivien . . . She stroked at my hair, and I submitted, lying back, bemused. How could I not have seen you?

'I often wondered. You ignored me utterly,' she teased, and I must have looked wounded, because then she laughed. 'Like I said, I sat at the back. You wore your glasses, to read your notes; I was at best a greyish blur, I expect.' Is there any knowledge so touchingly intimate as this – the limits of the vision of a spectacle-wearing spouse? And how quickly she has learned my range. Awful, to think of her sitting there, unseen. 'My own notes were hopeless, all over the page, I couldn't write fast enough to catch everything, and I couldn't bear to look away from you,' she went on. Why have you never said? I asked. Why did you never tell me, that you were sitting there, all the time? 'I was . . . I don't know. I was embarrassed,' she confessed. 'I didn't want you to think it was the only reason I'd chosen your class the next autumn.' But was that the reason, then?

She was blushing now, unless it was the warmth of the fire; I could smell her, warm salt-spice. A young woman's smell. I no longer sweat as I used to. Papery thin dry skin. Crimpy hair standing out like a wire brush when I lift my arm.

Was that the reason? I asked. 'Well, yes, sort of. I mean, not just because I liked you – I mean, *liked* you liked you . . .' I smiled. 'I *mean*, I liked your lectures. I was there in the first place because I liked the poems. I kept coming back to hear you read them. I liked the way you spoke, but also the things you said and the way you said them. When I went back to the page, I heard your voice. It was part of *why* I liked you.' Why you *liked* me liked me, I clarified. 'All right,' she conceded. 'Liked, *liked*, admired, adored.'

And now? I said. I am . . . what? Tolerated? Forborne? 'Oh, stop,' she said, with a little nuzzle-nudge. 'Now I just love you. No more . . . circumlocution.' Her fingers tracing circles on my temples.

'And then I went to your seminars and planned clever things to say days in advance and then didn't dare to say them half the time, and was furious when I did and they talked over me, those stupid know-all boys; I hated all the others,' she said, 'talking on and on; because I wanted you to know that I'd been thinking of you, of your class. Of you.' Those boys, I said, those fawning boys, always following, fussing about you; didn't you see? 'Not at all,' she said. 'I can't say I noticed at all. I loved you first; as Vivien says, that warps the wit.' She stroked my stubble. When did I last shave? How long have we been here? I wonder, shall I grow a great sagacious beard, for my retirement?

First, truly? I asked. I like to hear her say it. She merely smiled. She might be your kinswoman, I said, the Northumbrian princess. Merlin's last folly.

Tennyson's Vivien is a wilful, scheming, vengeful soul, who by her sulks and seductions at last deceives a melancholy Merlin into revealing the spell that will confine him. In other versions of the legend, under other names, it is Merlin who pursues her, who teaches her everything he knows, as a gift; whose obsessive, possessive love so exhausts her that at last, in a desperate bid to be free of him, she tricks him and traps him.

But she says it is neither one. 'I think old Alfred gets it wrong,' she said. 'It isn't so simple, it isn't just a power struggle. Why shouldn't they really be lovers?' So in her version they are complicit, she is his scribe and his student, and Merlin knows, knows from the start that he has doomed himself by giving her his heart; knows that she will outstrip him, and resigns himself to his fate. Almost as if he is simply tired, I said, and wants only a little love to warm him at the last, and is ready for his endless unseen sleep. 'Oh, stop,' she said. 'It's not time to sleep just yet.' She pressed upon my chest, pressed me down and lay beside me, one long thigh across my legs and her lips by my ear, murmuring, and tickling, and teasing. So will you, in the end, bewitch me, I asked? Will you leave your old teacher imprisoned, lost to life and use and name and fame? 'Well,' she said, considering me carefully. 'Will you yield?'

And she laughed her soft and mocking laugh, the laugh of a much older woman, rich in the ember darkness; and reached over my head to put her glass down, and I raised myself up to meet her and turn her under me but she eased me back down, a hand on my chest and the other stroking my brow.

Well, she may mock. Still there have been times, as I grew older and my hair greyed, that I wondered what I was waiting for; but now I know, now I know, I look up and she will be there on the beach, my nymph, my northern girl, my Niviane.

Wednesday

She saw a flood coming, in the night. I woke to a grasping, blind kiss, her mouth to mine as if to give or steal breath. Before I knew where I was or who, I knew her; already I grow accustomed. Her body, her mouth, her gasp.

I held her until she calmed. 'I was at the window and the tide was coming in, these huge waves coming closer and closer to the house, and there were silver fish, all leaping about in it, and . . . and goldfish too, bright orange against the green,' she said, and then laughed a little with the relief of the dreamer who, recalling the single absurd detail in the safety of waking, knows now for certain it was only a dream. 'The sea came right in and covered us, and the fish were all swimming around us, and we were all red and gold and silver, all scaly, and there were lights in the water like fireflies and I felt so . . . *lithe*, but then I saw' – and here she paused, catching her breath, lost in the torrent, and pressed her mouth on mine again, her fingers curling and tugging at the hair on my chest – 'you couldn't breathe! And when I realized it, I realized I couldn't either . . . and you were saying my name, trying to say my name, and . . .'

And it was just a dream, I said. Listen, I said, the sea is far off, and quiet. Shhhh, I said, stroking her hair until she gave in to the sleep that would erase all memory of her waking.

I have always been a deep and dreamless sleeper; it is unlike me to lie in late and drowse in the day. I have had many years of regular routine and unbroken rest. I must try not to resent the loss of this bachelor's privilege; I am glad to be beside her, staying close to the surface in case she needs me. If I could go into that ocean with her I would; I can at least be ready to hold her when she wakes. I listened to the sea all through the night, the sh-shhh-shhhh of it, consoling, and took a somnolent pleasure in thinking myself adrift with her on a raft in the shallows. My dreams, unlike hers, leave barely an impression and washed from me as I woke this morning, wanting her, savouring her warmth and the sound of her breathing before I reached for her and discovered she was already up, and there was no one there to reach for.

I found her in the kitchen, slicing bread at crazy angles. I boiled eggs. We sat at the table in a companionable silence; she bothered an old crossword, the last few clues of which have for days eluded us. She outlined the unfilled squares, over and over, each unsolved answer becoming ever more emphatically blank and funereally bordered. I had a vision of her then as she was in my seminar room, curved into her chair behind the fold-down desk flap, her left pen-hand curled covetous around her own page; her narrow wrist emerging from a striped open shirt cuff, the other cuff hanging long from her forearm. A man's shirt. It used to be her father's, she told me later (that elusive, long-armed man; did he abandon his whole wardrobe and flee?); at the time, I found myself wondering if she'd rolled into it out of some boy's bed that morning. Remembering those mornings long ago when I'd sat in a lecture hall, yawning, self-satisfied and smelling of sex. I wondered this, in fact, with a pang in the chest that I put down hopefully to the possible onset of angina. Because it couldn't be, at this time of life, nearing the peak of my moderately illustrious career, it couldn't be love. The thought was risible. And yet there she sat, right hand shoved into her tangled hair to hold her own head up like a trophy, Hercules and Medusa in one, and bent over the page, her long legs crossed at the ankle in front, short trousers and sandals revealing the long bones of her shins and feet (toes compressed together, hiding the webbing that I would much later discover). And I, watching the jut of her joints, I felt my heart burn and hoped it was only heartburn.

And yet, and yet, there she sat at our conjugal breakfast table, all these months later, in the very same pose, her curved wrist and hand as white, strong and vicious as a swan's neck, the pen stabbing at the page. 'Still stuck,' she said. Her pen spiralled in the margin, the line curling about itself in eddies. She filled the whole space with scrolling waves, working into the pattern so that it grew ever darker. An impenetrable mass of currents, contradicting. The side of her hand, as ever, smudged with biro. 'Give up,' she said, with a resigned smack of the pen on the table. 'We'll get it eventually.' And she yawned and stretched, having all the time in the world. It's the last clue, but I can't think what the word might be, either.

She turned her attention to her egg, dipping each toasted soldier with military precision. When the last of the white was scooped out, she quite suddenly plunged her teaspoon through the bottom of the shell, a resounding crack in the quiet kitchen. Then she reached over, took mine, and did the same. 'So the witches can't sail in them,' she explained. Another of her habits, added to the store.

'I had such a strange dream last night,' she said then. Did you, my darling? I asked.

It occurs to me that I think of us, when I imagine our life together, at a perpetual breakfast table, with a long, bright day ahead of us and no need to rush, all the long morning to listen to her dreams, to murmur 'pass the milk,' to ask 'another cup?', to mutter 'six letters, something O something O something something . . .', reading out clues in playful competition. But of course, come January and the new term, I shall have to rise early for work and leave her; these lazy breakfasts will have to be reserved for the weekends until, in a few years' time (not so very far off, now), the weekends will stretch out into a long, sun-filled retirement; a retreat from the world, she and I.

And why should she be ready to retire, before even entering the field? Might she not want to embark upon her own career? What does she mean to do with her future? That future ever encroaching, in only a few days' time . . . We are, it seems, avoiding such questions as, What shall we do? And how shall we live? Will she be content to make her home in my home, to cross the threshold for a last time and remain there? I try to imagine her, on my sofa, in my chair, at my sink drying my dishes – as I have seen her before – but it is a question of the word 'our' and how that might be accommodated. Is there space for a second desk in the study? Or will she take to the dining room table and cover it in papers? Or will she weed the garden and learn to bake? Unlikely. Will she fill the place with rocks and stones and shells and bones, and all the fragments she finds washed up on the shore?

I did ask her, once: where do you hope to be, a decade from now? Less than a month ago, yet it seems an age has passed since that moment of late summer madness – that moment when her answer made me ask her to marry me.

She arrived at my door one day at the end of August; a manu-
script illumination, bright against a cobalt sky. She arrived from
nowhere, without explanation. It had been a long, pointlessly hot
summer, numb and grey with her absence, with the knowledge
of her ongoing absence; the thought of the term, the year, the life
ahead – the lectures, the books, the staff dinners, the ceremonies –
all rendered meaningless, and hopelessly mundane. The thought
of class after class without her.

I had to assume she'd abandoned academia, and me. I'd sent
her an email but her university account had lapsed. And then
there she was, a miracle on my doorstep, as radiant as the day, as
if fallen out of the depthless blue heaven. 'I was passing,' she said.
'I thought I'd drop by. I'm glad I remembered the house. From
the party?' Ah, of course, I said, as if I had been wondering, as if I
could have forgotten it, that last time I'd seen her. I thought you'd
all gone home for the summer, I said. But you've decided to come
back? To study? 'Not sure yet. Thought I'd use the library while
I can,' she said. I invited her in, half-crazed, thinking the sun must
have made me delirious. My eyes adjusting to the dimness of the
hall and expecting to find her resolved into a shadow, a delusion, a
trick of the light. But there she was, apparently substantial. Where
have you been all summer? I asked her. 'Nowhere in particular,'
she said. 'Aestivating. I burn easily.' I have still not quite deter-

mined where it is she was hiding; where exactly is nowhere? In any case, from out of it, out of a blue nowhere, she came to my door that Tuesday, and we drank tea in the garden and talked poetry. That Friday, I bumped into her at the library – that is, I lay in wait for three days, haunting the stacks, until I found her – and we went to a café in town. I watched her crumble a piece of carrot cake to crumbs, and stick them back together and eat it a pinch at a time. She went ahead of me when we left, I reached around her awkwardly to open the door, there was a near collision in which we didn't quite touch. Then I didn't see her for days, and I realized I had no means of reaching her. She made no further appearance at the library and I fretted and moped, and then there she was on my doorstep again. I invited her in. We drank white wine this time – I think she brought a bottle with her, or perhaps it was I that broached it; in any case, it was after six o'clock, and a mellow, liquid evening, meant to be filtered through a glass as the shadows lengthen. A draught of vintage, tasting of flora and the country-green; O for a beaker full of the warm South! I cried, as the last drops went down. 'That I might drink, and leave the world unseen,' she said . . . and, for the first time, her hand brushed my arm. I lay in bed that night, my own hand gripping the bare dry skin where her cold fingers had been.

And then there she was another day, and another, always unannounced: a series of portraits framed in the doorway, the same pose recurring, with a bottle of wine, with leaves in her hair, with the rain running off her, with spaghetti and sauce. Where have you been? What have you been up to? I would ask; and she'd say 'here and there' or 'this and that', arresting lightly all further enquiry. How easily she seems to slide the past from her shoulders like that. The future, too. And the present is only precariously balanced, and might dislodge at any moment.

I began to dread going out, in case I should miss her. I began to stock up on groceries – potted shrimp, antipasti, good bread, figs – that I could throw together into the semblance of a simple, yet sophisticated, impromptu supper for two. One Wednesday she arrived with a bag of shopping and made terrible, overcooked, salty pasta and, as we sat twirling it on our forks into one sticky, gluti-nous lump almost too heavy to lift, she suggested that perhaps I could teach her to cook, and I blustered and said there was no need, this was delicious, and she said I was sweet and leaned across and kissed me on the cheek and almost tipped over in the flimsy garden chair, righting herself with a bang and a laugh. For a second I felt it, her soul's warmth on my cheek in the cooling evening; I am sure that this happened, however unlikely. Unless it was I that gave her that first quick peck, in gratitude and after too much wine, bidding farewell at my door one evening. In any case it became our habit to embrace, briefly, and exchange brief kisses on meeting and parting, as friends do. As an old ex-student might her tutor, after years of supervision. And yet she'd never been demonstrative with any other person, so far as I had seen; and I found myself suspecting, hoping, and having to quell at every touch this unthinkable hope.

Once, she took my arm as we walked through the town, and saw Dr Jones, who'd taught her Jacobean drama in her second year; he nodded and failed not to stare as we passed, but she only hooked on tighter, linking her hands. And once, as we lay on the grass outside the library, taking a break, looking up through the deepening beech leaves, dappled, dazed in the green light, I asked what she'd been working on that day, and she said Browning, and we talked for a while about transience and half-rhyme, and then she was quiet for a time and I turned to see her eyes closed, the green-veined lids, and longing to kiss her cheek I murmured, I pluck the rose, and love it more than tongue can speak; and she sighed a little with her eyes still closed as if she might be sleeping, and smiled. 'No need to speak,' she said. I thought I had been subtle; she says now that I might as well just have kissed her. But that kiss is sweeter still in memory for remaining unkissed.

That was the night we went to dinner, and she licked lobster from her fingers, and then licked mine.

That, at least, is how I remember it. She won't have it. You licked my finger, I told her last night. Remember? You took my finger to your lips and licked it.

'You put your finger on my mouth,' she said, indignant. 'I said, you're only sixty, and you said hush and put your finger on my lips and I licked it.' No, I said, no, you took my hand and drew it to you. 'No, you hushed me. You reached over the table and said hush, and your finger tasted of butter so I licked it.' Of butter? 'We'd been eating lobster, remember?' We? 'We shared a lobster. I wanted to watch you eat so I'd know how to. So I wouldn't make a mess.' She looked down, away. She was quiet for a moment, chewing a hang-nail, sitting on the end of the bed in her nightie; and then: 'But I think I've made a mess anyway,' she blurted. 'Just look at the mess I've got you in to. Is it going to be awful for you when you go back? Will they say nasty seedy things about you?' I expect they will, I said, trying not to sound pleased. 'Well, you've only yourself to blame,' she said.

My life was far too tidy anyway, I said. I couldn't care less what they say about me, you know that. I shall revel in the mess. I couldn't be happier, stranded here, cast adrift on the edge of the world without a library, without resources, without an internet connection, worn out by your dreams and your demands, getting nothing done. However, I teased, if there were a blame to be apportioned, I would blame you. You came to me, I reminded her. You called me Richard, you came to my house, you licked my finger. She said, wide-eyed, 'I was innocent until you put your finger to my lips. Until you touched me. Until I tasted you.' I hushed her; she opened her mouth and closed it over my thumb.

But she dissembles. I could not possibly have forgotten it, how she took my hand and twisted. How she appeared from nowhere in my office, in my garden, at my door. Otherwise how could I possibly have been so bold?

No matter: after the lobster, a week later, or a few days later, I promised her the sea if she would marry me. A day of unde-served sunshine, a last warm dreg of the season, with the faintest freshness of a new one in the breeze. A coolness in the shade that hadn't been there a week before. So what are your plans, I asked. What do you mean to do with your year? Where, in ten years, do you hope to be? I pulled up grass and dropped it on her belly, like a teenager. She threaded daisies into chains with her quick long fingers. She said, 'With you.' With that flush at her temple, the bright dark depth of her eyes when they meet mine entirely, she said: 'Reading. Working with you. I don't know, anything; but with you.' Oh, my sweet girl. And what shall we do, and where shall we go? I said, making a game of it, not wanting to break this precious hint of a promise. 'Anywhere. I don't care. Near the sea.' Is that all? I asked. 'Just you, and a sea view,' she said. And then? I did not ask – and then and then? And after then? After I am seventy, after I am eighty? I didn't ask, and still, I do not ask this. Instead, at the time, without a moment's forethought, I asked her to marry me.

I split a daisy, carefully, carefully, and pulled it through itself to make a ring, and offered it to her, to complete the set – she was already crowned and garlanded, a faery queen, and I her swarthy Oberon. She splayed her left hand and smiled when I chose her ring finger. I kneeled before her. 'Do you mean it?' she asked. If you do, I said; I've gone mad, I thought. Of course she doesn't. 'You want to stay with me?' I do, I said, light-headed. 'You love me?' she asked. So she made me ask three times, to seal the spell. I do, of course I do. I kissed her, at last. She kissed me. The low sun, the gold light, her silver hair, her eyes. Vertiginous, unreal.

We lay on the riverbank like old-fashioned lovers. 'Courting' she called it, 'it's still called courting, where I was brought up. That's what my mam would say, if I told her.' I've no idea what her mother did say, when she did tell her, if she did; I haven't exchanged a single word with the woman. I wanted to ask for her hand, but she wouldn't hear of it. She said it was already her own, to give as she pleased. That was the last we spoke of it.

So it was that last Friday morning, she arrived at my door once again, bundled and belted into her coat, to cover her dress until the ceremony; bad luck, she said, for me to see it. She arrived with everything she owns, she said, dumping it all down in the middle of the sitting room. All her worldly goods: three meagre bags and a box of books. Two of the bags also full of books. My little ascetic. No ornaments or photographs, no keepsakes. No jewellery but for the ring on a silver chain around her neck, soon to be joined by the second, and now the jawbone talisman. She has no love of adornment.

She shooed me out of my own house and made me wait at the registry office in town for twenty minutes, and as each one of those minutes passed I felt a greater fool, until I had convinced myself that she would never turn up, had never intended to; I imagined myself returning home jilted, jagged, drunk. I'd reel in the door to find – what? An empty coat like a discarded chrysalis; everything precious robbed, the bookshelves bare. And I wouldn't even care.

And as the minute hand ticked the last minute and some-where a church bell chimed, as I turned in the direction of the pub I'd already picked out to drown my shame and sorrow in, there she suddenly was, in silk, shivering, her hair combed out straight and long, toenails red on her bare feet (was she barefoot? Surely not). When we tumbled giddily home that afternoon, I found a pile of her clothes on the sofa, make-up a clutter on the sink; she'd ranged her little library on the shelves, alongside my own, stowing books lengthways on top where they wouldn't fit and leaving little stacks along the mantel.

And now she is waiting for me on the shore. She is looking out to sea, but she is waiting for me. I am meant to be working but it is again a bright, braa day as they say here, the water glinting in the cold clear air, the sea-mist aglitter with the sunlight that glitters too in her hair, and half an hour ago, as I took my place here, she knocked shyly on the open door to the living room and said we should go for a walk, a picnic, today. I accepted the invitation with alacrity. It is a pleasantly novel sensation, an indulgent sort of guilt, to leave my desk and let my schedule slide. I see what a creature of habit I've become, having nobody to answer to, no other soul to accommodate; and old men are creatures of habit. So I said I would just finish up here but instead I'm just watching her, remembering, making her wait.

I will simply refuse to grow old. She who has bewitched my heart must surely have some spell to preserve me. My Nimue. She, at least, will never age. Or at least, I will never see her aging, which amounts to the same; wrinkled and fallen, hair fading, eyes dulled. No, I shall live perhaps just long enough to see the corners of her eyes crinkle with the years of laughing, that line between her brows deepen just a little with care, with crosswords; her hair no longer quite so remarkable, not quite so incongruous, ripened to the shade of a barley husk. Yes, I will perhaps see the onset of autumn; that is all. But the pale green veins I trace from collar to breast, from finger to wrist, from sternum to clavicle and back, so close to the surface of her skin – they will not burst or clot or swell or purple. My fingers follow the meander of them, like a network of underground rivulets, meeting, joining, branching. With a fingertip or the tip of my tongue I follow the long river running from the back of her knee, winding up inside her thigh and into the hollow of her, where her salt blood is hottest. Listening to the beat and ebb of her pulse, eddying out to her chilly extremities and swirling back into the hidden, unknown depths, the strong and secret currents of her heart.

*

I have spent the afternoon stretched out on tartan, on a cliff-top, with my wife beside me and a hamper, a thermos; holidaymakers from a bygone decade when I was a child and she years from conception in thought or deed. How far I have come, how long it has been since those awkward afternoons of my youth. We were not a convivial family. We would sit on our worn beach towels for as few hours as seemed mandatory, maintaining a gritty silence behind our respective reading matters of choice (wind-torn broad-sheet, hardback history from the library, orange Penguin). And now on this northern shore, far from any dirty old striped-awning beach on the south coast of England, although we do not bask in bathing suits, although we are well-wrapped and woolly and her nose pink with the frost in the air, how broad and new and possible life seems. The wide-winged grey-white birds all about us, soaring over, rising on the air and rounding, crying and dipping for a flash of silver, the bright, crisp sunshine, the shush of the waves, and our blanket between us and the scoured grass.

The path rises up, up from the cottage and then rubs itself out; we climbed over scrubby, warreny, rabbit- and sheep-soiled grass and nubbins of dried out sea-flowers, which seem to imitate the spongy sea corals below – far below, ever farther below. We walked a good way, she striding and skittering up the steeper sections, and I following after, trying not to puff, my eyes watering easily in the wind. Then, just as we could climb no further, we came to a great square chunk hewn out of the cliff, a geo she called it, with a hard g, a word from an ancient language that she half-knows or understands.

I went first, trying to reassure her, but a metre away from that fatal drop, swaying with the wind and dizziness, I dropped to my knees and went on all fours until one trembling hand, then the other, reached the sharp-cut edge, and I brought my head between them and looked down, down into that deep well, the land incised by a dark fissure, running with unseen torrents of fresh water hurtling hundreds of feet into the salt sea. I turned back to see her bravely crawling until she laid herself out beside me; summoning my last scraps of courage, I lifted my hand from the solid rock to close it over hers. High, black-grey-white banded cliffs, the sea crashing below, rushing through a long-eroded archway and white-whirling against the dark rocks; birds perched on every tiny ledge, and at the very top, the two of us clinging, daring ourselves and each other to look down. The sea boomed and bellowed in that echo chamber, gathering secret, hidden force under its surface to crash against the rocks in a great spout. I felt the spray of it on my cheek. Watching her watching, I saw her face transformed, at once fearful and compelled, so that I hardly knew her, her eyes as crazed and fathomless as the depths below, her mouth a little parted as if with desire.

She turned to me, breathless. 'Look,' she said, 'there in the centre where it's still: turquoise, emerald; and where the waves rise, the inside of them, dark, almost black, but . . .' Obsidian, I said. A sheen like cut stone. 'Yes!' she said. 'Like an old knife.' And then when they peak, sapphire, 'into azure, into aquamarine . . .' And all dissolving into foam, scouring out the caves below, or rushing through the narrow channel of the arch, or dashed again and again against the rocks, which seem now so immutable but will in time give way, give in, and be carried off by that same sea to become sand for some other distant shore.

We raised ourselves with care, taking very small slow steps away from the edge as if vertigo might hurl us over. 'My legs are shaking,' she said, and I put an arm around her shoulder and drew her close and kissed her woolly-hatted head, and did not say that I, too, was a little awestruck, a little terrified, and glad of her strong frame to lean on, feeling again the height of her, feeling bowed and humbled and trying to unclench my spine. We walked on, the ground again descending, until we came to the jut of a precipice that seemed comfortingly low and gentle in comparison to the cliff's height, with a substantial grassy patch upon which to make camp a comfortable six feet from the edge.

I had thought we were the only ones foolish enough to venture here for a holiday in this inhospitable season, but no. Below us, on the pebbled bay that the cliff face embraces, a family: two roistering teenage boys, their father in well-worn hiking gear, the mother just about bearing up. They were bird-watching on the opposite cliffs; I watched them pick out a treacherous path down the stepped stone and scrub, the boys goatish, skidding and hopping with all the invulnerable stupidity of adolescence, the father doing his best to keep up, already outstripped by his sons, anxiously gripping his binoculars against his tub of a belly. Their mother bringing up the rear step by hesitant, quavering step, clutching the rocks with one hand, the other left to grasp at hat, scarf, handbag all at once, in a dance of agitation. Now they have reached the shore. The boys throw stones, as boys do, into the water. It is, really, a marvellous day: the sea dark blue and no doubt freezing in the depths, and empty all the way to Greenland or the end of the earth, cloudless out to the horizon; no other colours in the world but silver and blue, the deep sea and the bright of her hair. I lie on my belly, propped on my elbows, ignoring the twinge at the base of my back, watching her. She is at the cliff's edge now, a hand shading her half-closed eyes, scrying the sky as the birds wheel and cry above her. She says that seagulls are the souls of dead sailors. Their cries seem to speak of fearsome seas: 'look-away, look-away' they seem to cry, and she does not.

Perhaps she will tell me, later, what they told her.

The father skims a stone across the sea, which comes in flat and placid in the shallows of the cove; the boys pretend that they are not impressed and go on with their graceless lobbing, but I see them five minutes later, when their father's back is turned, trying their skill at the same game, until the older one, with an elegant twirl, bounces his missile five, six, seven, eight times and cannot restrain a victory shout. The father turns, and they reassume postures of boredom; one shoves the other, half-heartedly, on the shoulder. The mother is sitting on a flat rock, with a book open unread on her lap. She turns and looks up at us, staring shamelessly. How much can she see of us, I wonder? I believe, from down there, we would make a handsome pair, if I were to stand and join my wife now. Tall. Refined. Silver and tin. There is a breeze stirring, coming in off the sea; the tide, I think, is advancing. It will be up to that woman's ankles, soon. It is almost three o'clock. I think I shall open our wine. I think I will pour two glasses and go to the cliff's edge and make a show of toasting my beautiful young wife, and pull her shawl tight around her, and linger over the salt on her lips.

I wish I could preserve her, just as she is this afternoon; but when I try to take her picture, she whisks her shawl in front of her face like an exotic dancer – a Salome dressed in jeans and long socks and vests and jumpers, layer upon layer over her nakedness. In every photograph I have ever taken of her, she has looked away, or shaken her head, or run beyond the frame even, so that I could compile an entire album of phantoms, of nondescript backgrounds peopled by silver glimpses, by smears of semi-features, by the white flash of a vanishing ankle against an otherwise unremarkable stone wall. The first time, it was evening, a slow late summer evening that we had whiled away at a bar by the river; a peaceful, scented, drowsy evening, a deep gold light fading, calling for a long exposure. But when I took the shot she turned her head to look out at the water glittering behind her, so that all I caught was the blur of her turn and behind her, an unfocused swan. She doesn't object or grow angry when I point the camera. Sometimes she makes a play of sitting quite still, posing, pouting, and at the last minute ducking, diving, hiding. It has become a game, catch me if you can. What I would give to make a portrait, a record, to capture every nuance, her guises, her guilelessness; to attempt to exhaust the inexhaustible store of her variety in a single likeness. To make of this moment a keepsake – so that I am able to recall, one Wednesday five or twenty years from now, how on this now long-past afternoon she was thus: her sleeves thrust up, ink on her fingers, a hand to her brow as she reads the horizon. As if she will not outlive me, which of course she shall, by many years; as if I will one day, in the agony and the emptiness of her permanent absence, have need of such paltry morsels.

But at this moment, even if she could be persuaded to be still for a second, the light is changing all the time as dusk comes, the sky racing and dancing with new clouds knotting themselves out of vapour, now pale grey, now lambent, now dissolving into the sun-soaked blue, like her eyes, and the portrait would bear no resemblance to this afternoon's memory, even as it forms and fades.

Thursday

'Let's have some more stories, then,' she said last night as we lay by the fire, guzzling wine. 'I want to know more about these magical women of yours, getting all the attention.' If only she knew it is quite the reverse – how my mind is irresistibly drawn out to her on the shore . . . I trawled for something to tell her. Tales of sea-serpents. Beautiful Lamia, who only wanted to be alone with her love, exposed to the cruel eyes of Apollonius' reason and revealed in all her awful glory, shining, pale, dumb; her Lycius, besotted, who would show off his prize, and die for the loss of it. Melusine, denounced by her husband as a water-snake before his court; in despair, transformed, forsaken, unable to change back, she leaps from his battlements into the ocean. Both twisted into coils by the word, by being named serpent. Foolish French Raymond, senseless Lycius. Why not let it lie . . .

It seems I effected some transfiguration, for she woke with a wet thrash in the night and said she'd been swimming in her sleep, long-tailed; she'd fallen or flown from the cliff-top before the flood could reach and take her, and turned in the air and twisted into a limbless rope and plunged in a long dart through the sea, through the weeds and corals, down to where it's dark and she shone in the murk, she said. 'I was silver, shining, scaly,' she said. 'And I swam through the dark, and there were weeds trailing on me, and then something grabbed me and I tried to break free, but I'd lost my tail and I couldn't swim or breathe any more at all. And I woke up.' She was breathless still, her heartbeat hard against me, but she seemed exhilarated as much as she was frightened and pulled me to her as much as she clung; an urgency in her voice and hands and mouth which I could do nothing to resist. The strength of her, her long legs and arms around me . . . She twisted around and beneath me and I held fast to her as she thrashed.

I lay awake until I was sure she was peaceful, drifting contented beside her, feeling the cooling of our spent heat; I think I dreamed of fishes.

I was woken late by a prod in the ribs from her sharp and insistent toe. I was face down, sprawled, I fear slack-jawed – the pillow under my cheek was wet. I opened one eye to see her by the bedside, performing a curious ballet, one prodding leg extended while she balanced a tray in her hands. 'I made coffee!' she said. 'And toast!' My first breakfast in bed with her. 'I burned the toast a bit,' she said. 'But I scraped it off.' That scent in the air, acrid and yet somehow homely. She clambered in beside me and we crunched in contented silence. I yawned between mouthfuls. 'Did you sleep badly?' she said through her last mouthful. A little, I said. You? 'I don't know, I was having weird dreams again . . .' Yes, I said. I remember. 'Oh . . . did I wake you?' she said. 'Sorry.' I don't mind, I said; but I am starting to wonder if I'll ever sleep through the night again. Have you always had these nightmares? I asked. She made a non-committal noise and rolled over onto me, lifting the plate to the floor in one motion. Her mouth tasted of burnt toast crumbs and butter.

The sea is lively and inviting this morning and splashes up the beach, reaching for her, whispering brightly. She is out there already. She is building, I think, a sort of primitive castle, not unlike the ancient brochs left abandoned all about these isles. Lacking tools and manpower, she is simply hollowing the sand with two cupped palms onto a growing tower, which she smoothes and rounds as she goes. It is emerging less as a castle than as a single turret, Elaine building her own prison to await her Lancelot. Existing only in a mirror, all the world shrouded, half-sick of shadows. The low winter sun casts them long on the beach.

Yes, there, she has formed rough battlements for the roof and drawn down a single long window in one side. Now she beds in bands of seashells, patiently fortifying her walls with purple shards and shining stones and sea-smoothed glass. Intent upon her task; as precise and careful as a child.

I grew up near the sea. Have I told her that? Not near enough to walk to; but we had a car, and my father would drive us, the three of us, on summer weekends, until by the end of every August I had accumulated a shoe-box full of half-eaten sticks of rock, carefully kept for later. Each one with my name struck right through the centre, 'RICHARD', revealing itself as a streak of blue beneath the pink where I'd sucked off the coating; and this sticky log pile growing stickier by the week and finally, alarmingly furred over with a fluorescent green mould of a hue that no organic thing would ever take upon itself to cultivate. An acid taste at the back of my tongue, now.

I would build complex sandcastles, armouring the walls with cockleshells and the long, much-prized razor clams; how sprawling and crenellated those ramparts, in comparison to hers. All pomp and ceremony, and animated with imagined pageants. I would dig a moat and then a channel so that the incoming sea would fill it, and then sit down safe within my fortifications in the forecourt, looking out at the approaching tide. The solitary sea-king of the castle.

Eventually it would be time to go for fish and chips. And later, looking out from the car as we drove along the front, sucking on my stick of rock, I would try to find my castle there on the sand; so great a citadel I had built that it must surely be visible from the road, from space perhaps. But there was never any sign, not so much as a tattered and lonely pennant, all that splendour already washed out by the tide.

And now she is standing . . . And quite without warning, has lifted her skirt, drawn back her high-booted foot, and kicked the tower down in a gleeful little dance that makes me laugh, although I can't say if it's for my benefit. She stands with her hands on her hips, admiring the wreckage of her own handiwork. The tilt of her chin is triumphant; soon those sorry ruins, too, will be effaced.

*

I went out to her at lunchtime and found her flat on her back on the sand as if sleeping, a picture of repose, her palms turned up and eyelids only just closed, quivering; as I drew nearer she opened her eyes and said, 'Hello, Richard,' although I was sure I had made no sound. I moved closer, until my shadow covered her. What are you up to? I said. 'Just listening to the water, enjoying the sunlight,' she said. 'I'm just happy, playing in the sand.' I liked your tower, I said. 'I kicked it down before the tide could take it.' Yes, I saw, I said.

She sat, and ruffled her hair, rimed and sea-stained and raggedy, her skin salt-stung, her hair stuck with damp sand; strands of fine seaweed clung to her clothes, the miraculous survivor of a wreck. I told her so. She said, 'Oh, brave new world, that hath such creatures in it!' But you are more, perhaps, the sprite, I mused; my tricksy capricious Ariel; 'and you the wizard that freed me?' Yes, better. But . . . 'into willing bondage,' she assured. 'Don't you worry about that. I'm all yours,' she said, taking my proffered hand and allowing me to pull her up before giving a little curtsey and planting a briny kiss. 'Your willing servant.' And she laughed.

Very well. Let me play the old conjuror. Let us raise a tempest about us; only let us be alone, our own island. But no. Even this barren place, here at the world's end, is far too populous. We have had a regrettably sociable afternoon.

I said I was going to the shop. 'I could come with you,' she said, putting an arm through mine and setting off at a happy jog. She wanted to buy 'some stuff'. What sort of stuff? I asked. I can get it for you. 'I don't know, really,' she said. 'I just thought I'd have a poke about.'

I felt strangely reluctant to subject her to Mr Begg's inspection, as if he might be some Orcadian Apollonius, coldly unweaving rainbows in his back room; but I could hardly say no. I can't lock her in, or chain her to a rock. So we sauntered along the road to the little town; or rather, she sauntered, I trudged.

As I feared, the ting of the shop's bell drew the keeper from his cavern, and while she 'poked about' his hoard, oblivious, his hard eyes never left her: this sprightly, bright young woman in a chunky woollen hat, the glint of her teeth as she smiled. He watched her as she turned over this and that: picking over the fruit and taking an apple; opening tins and boxes of paints and settling for a soft sketching pencil and a pad of cartridge paper; testing a lipstick from the small cosmetics stand on the back of her hand, eventually selecting a scarlet one that made her look, at the hotel bar this evening, positively vampiric, positively wanton, in a way I find both unsettling and arousing. My red-mouthed virgin Lamia . . .

She approached the counter with her haul and set it down, then scanned the jars of sweets behind the counter, biting her lower lip with her crooked tooth, taking her time, Mr Begg staring all the while. Only when she had asked for a bag of 'soor plums' in an impressive, and I think unconscious, Scots accent, and he had measured them out, scarcely taking his eyes off her; only when he had given the bag his practised little twist at both corners, and rung through her other choices, along with the ground coffee and bottles of wine I'd picked up, did they both turn to me expectantly, like allies. 'That's thirty-nine pounds thirty, then,' he said. I took out my wallet and handed over two notes. 'I've got the thirty!' she chirped, and dropped two silver coins into his hand, produced from some mysterious pocket in the many folds of her clothing. In turn, he placed a pound coin in her palm, with unnecessary deliberation, I thought, so that his rough fingertip must have grazed her skin. 'Have a good day!' she called as we left. 'Aye,' he nodded.

Outside, she offered me a sweet from her little bag. 'I just made seventy pence off you, it's the least I can do,' she said. 'You don't have to buy me things. But thank you.' I wonder how many silver pieces she has secreted about her person. I've never seen her with a purse. My pleasure, I said, or almost said, the end of the word coming out as a cough as I choked on a slew of acidic saliva. These are terrible, I said. 'I know!' she said cheerily. 'My dad used to buy them when I was little, for a treat. He used to have them when he was a bairn, he said.' And felt that he should visit the same punishment upon successive generations? I asked. 'Maybe,' she said. And shrugged, and crumpled the bag closed and off she skipped. These curious scraps of herself that she offers, just as quickly snatched back.

I caught up to her and we set out for home; the sun was setting, pale yellow like chilled, smooth-churned butter behind new pleats of cloud. Leaning on each other, a little giggly with sugar. When we reached our turning, I suggested instead we

continue along the road to the hotel for a drink. She looked
dubious; the night was frosting over, closing in. But I was keen,
suddenly, to have her on my arm, to show her in society, such as
it is in these circumscribed parts, and she complied.

We walked with our arms wound around each other, as if
taking part in a three-legged race, lagging hopelessly ever further
behind as we grew ever more entangled. By the time we'd reached
the hotel, a fifteen-minute walk, it was almost dark. We arrived
a jolly pair, bursting through the door of the lounge, bringing
the chill in with us and quickly shutting it behind. The sudden
enclosure of an ordinary room, of carpets and curtains and electric light, which we had seen from afar as we walked, growing
brighter by the minute as the dusk crept in. There are no lights
on the roads, here, and coming in from the night I felt like some
mediaeval interloper, a pilgrim, eyes adjusting to a new, futuristic
world. Although this was not quite even the present, perhaps;
not as we know it. I shouldn't think a great deal has changed
in that room for thirty years or more: the wallpaper, the boxy
TV, the dusty fake flowers on the mantel, the choice of drinks —
some of the bottles themselves, I shouldn't wonder, those exotic
untouched spirits growing sticky, syrupy, clagged with dust. It
was hot, stifling after the snap of the outside air, and she pulled
off her hat, flushed, eyes bright, her mouth startling red with the
lipstick I had not seen her apply.

The family we saw on the cliffs were sitting at the largest of the five tables; their conversation halted as we came in, turning and nodding a hello before turning back inwards. Perhaps they hadn't been talking in the first place. The mother staring vacantly at the switched-off television in the corner; the father, still in his pocketed combat-green body warmer, scrolling through pictures on an impressive digital SLR, quite incongruous in that environment, like the technology of a distant age. The boys, as before, sullen, offering the occasional grunt when their father held out the screen to show them. The bar was unattended, but within a minute or so a woman appeared from a door marked 'Reception', and nodded to us as she took her place behind it. Neatly turned out in a white blouse and black skirt, blocky heels, blocky ankles, and a face like a soor plum. The father rose to buy more drinks; his glass perhaps had been empty some time. 'Evening,' he said. 'Chilly out, isn't it? What'll you have? Can I offer you and your . . .' He looked at her properly then, the usual masked surprise, not staring but glancing over her again, her eyes, her skin, and her silver hair, her scarlet lips; 'your . . . what are you drinking?' I introduced myself, and pointedly, my wife. He said his name was Jim, or something like that. I wasn't listening. I was trying to silently convey, in answer to the urgent non-expression behind my wife's clouded eyes, my apologies. We couldn't say no. It would have seemed rude, to keep apart from them in what was more or less a sitting room. After five long seconds or so of this unspoken stand-off she managed a smile and asked for a gin and tonic. I said I'd have a Highland Park and he said he'd have the same. The landlady nodded approvingly. Her scowl returned, quite rightly, when he asked for ice. I helped him carry the drinks over and we pulled up rickety dining chairs to join them. Hers was especially crooked; she rocked, gently, from the front left leg to the right back, as if on a ship, quietly creaking. There was an exchange of handshakes and greetings followed by half a minute's awkward silence.

'What a week for weather, eh?!' exclaimed Bill suddenly. Or Jim, was it. 'I've been to this place in all seasons and it's always the same, sunshine one minute and chucking down the next; and the wind! I should hang on to that slender wife of yours, Richard, she'll be blown away!' His elder son blushed. His wife hid a frown. My slender wife made her red mouth smile in a way I am glad I have not seen before. It would be a terrible thing, to have that smile turned on me.

'What brings you two here in October?' he asked then. Our honeymoon, I said. 'Lucky you,' he said to my wife sarcastically, as if I'd dragged her here by the hair to satisfy some perversion, when we could have been sunning ourselves in the Algarve or wherever people like him expect honeymooners to sun themselves. 'My fault, actually,' she said. 'I wanted to come here.'

What on earth for, they didn't ask. And yourselves? I asked instead. 'For the birds,' he said, and actually winked. I thought I heard the older son mutter 'Oh, God.' 'I'm a birder. It's a great place for it. The sandpipers were out on the rocks today. And we spotted some Greenland geese the other day, didn't we . . .' he said, to no member of his family in particular, it seemed. I wondered how long this monologue might go on for, at what point it might become a slide-show – he seemed the type, he was fidgeting with the camera, and I saw his son glance balefully at it. 'And the shrikes are flocking, too . . .'

'So, how did you two meet?' interrupted Linda, with the rudeness that only years of marriage can breed. How often, as a confirmed bachelor, I observed it and sneered. But no, we'll never stale into sniping and contempt, I can't imagine it. And besides we haven't the time, we haven't the luxury of years . . .

These thoughts do tend to creep up on me, in her absence. Sitting in my chair like an invalid in pyjamas. She is clattering around in the kitchen, from whence I have been banished; there is a salty savoury steam in the air and salt on my mouth, from hers. I am listening to her humming to herself and to my own heart slow, recuperating – she has just lately risen from my lap – the beat of it brittle within the hollow murmur of the sea . . . I inhale, exhale, hearing the tide out there in the dark. Brittle heart beating.

It seems foolish to spend a beat of it anywhere away from her, to waste a moment of marriage when there may not be many remaining. How long can it last?

Enough of that.

'I think we saw you, yesterday, on the cliffs,' said Linda – this apparent non-sequitur a way of making known that she had observed already that we are lovers. I wanted you to see, I thought. I saw you watching. And maybe you're thinking now, an older man . . . a man like that, with broad shoulders and big hands, and a little experience, would know what to do with me.

But again I digress. And would much prefer not to think of my hands upon thwarted, bitter-mouthed, stout little Linda, dressed up for the evening in a horrid pink blouse.

We were thrown together, I said, in the fruitiest tone I could muster – why not play the role? – by the gods of pedagogy. The younger boy stifled a snigger, at a nudge from his smirking brother. 'By . . . ?' said Linda. 'At university,' my wife cut in hurriedly. 'That's how we met. I went to his lectures. I graduated this summer.' We were married just a few days ago – well after her graduation, I said soothingly. I'm on sabbatical this term. 'Oh, a sabbatical. Yes, I see,' said Linda, not at all sure that she did. The older boy taking an interest now, I thought; sipping his half-pint of cider and watching her from under long faun's lashes. Pretty in a way that will be featureless when he's grown. Not her type, I nearly snarled.

The father, too, clearly fascinated, leering out of the corner of his eye at her; envious, no doubt, and determined to maintain his position as alpha male, as *paterfamilias* – and wishing perhaps that Linda hadn't worn that blouse, or was another woman entirely. In the fuggy heat of the room, my wife had pulled off her coat and the voluminous sweater that she has stolen from me to slouch about in, revealing a wide-necked green top that shows off her collarbones, her long neck, stretched now as she turned up the perfect, cat-sharp V of her jaw, echoed by the chain pulled out taut from her throat as she dragged the rings on it from side to side distractedly, scanning the bookshelves that ran about the room at picture-rail height and evidently finding nothing of interest.

'What Uni?' asked the older boy abruptly, and blushed; 'I'm applying this year.' This boy who seemed to me a child, I realized, is almost her contemporary; only a few years between them, born in the same decade. Being seventeen must be fresh, to her, whereas to me it is merely a notion, an age that I must assume happened to me, once. I watched him, sipped my whisky, tried to mask my irritation at this attempt to form an alliance of youth against balding decrepitude (the balding, at least, only on Bob's part. I raked a hand through my hair). I wondered if she'd take up the offer. But she answered dismissively, glancing at him only for a moment, offhand.

'Oh, yeah,' he said. 'I was thinking about going there. But it's a bit, uh, a bit *rah*, isn't it?' he asked, pleased with himself. 'A bit,' she said. 'I went there for the course. It had a good reputation.' A pause. The silence strained further. Ice cubes stirred with a straw. And then, out of boredom or kindness, she asked: 'What are you thinking of studying?' 'Uh, biology,' he said, the dark blotches of blush spreading. 'Right,' she said. 'You like plants. Or animals. You like life, or looking at it. Slides and cells and microscopes. Or is there more to it?' She was smiling, in a way that could have been encouraging or cruel, and for a moment I felt sorry for the boy, who seemed unsure if she had asked him a real question. 'I've been trying to get him interested in the birds, haven't I, Mart?' said his father, loudly. 'But he's got more of an eye for the pondlife.' 'Oh,' she said. 'Plenty of that about on campus.' And she went back to studying the spines of the books. So cool; in his sense of the word as well as mine, perhaps. Pale, detached.

How she strode, through the high columned forecourt of the library; in that hall of marble, how she shone. I rarely saw her in a crowd; even with her classmates, even in the midst of chattering, she was never link-armed, never a casual clasp of the arm or a squealing hug – she was set apart. They flittered and skulked around her, and she remained remote, aloof, tall, unacknowledged; how she shone.

'So . . . what about you?' said the boy to his half-pint glass. 'What did you study?'

'Yes, what is it you teach?' said Bob, to me, almost speaking over him. My wife turned to me, eyebrows raised, in mock-deferral. I allowed a dignified pause and said, grandly: Literature. Nineteenth century. Romantic to Victorian. It was Tennyson, I believe, that drew her to the lecture hall. 'Tennyson, eh? That what tickled you?' he said knowingly, as if this meant something – speaking as if to a precocious, just-budding girl. I believe he winked again. I wondered if she would like me to hit him. But no need, I think, for me to play monkeys.

'"In Xanadu, did Kubla Khan, a stately pleasure dome decree . . ."' he declaimed. Sitting back smugly. Looking about his family as if for applause, his eye at last resting, again, on my wife. 'Close enough,' she said, coolly, with a smile for me. He continued to look at her, a little discomfited now. A light went on, somewhere in a dusty schoolroom in the dim recesses of Linda's mind. 'Isn't that Coleridge? "Where Alf, the sacred river ran . . ."' (She most certainly said Alf. I could see her thinking, funny name for a river, that. Bit old-fashioned. Like Fred.) Well, yes, I said.

But I teach that, too, sometimes, I said, to reassure old Barry that he was right, in a way, after all. Amazingly, he bought it, and took a complacent sip from his icy dram. There was a companionable silence. '"Through caverns measureless to man, down to a sunless sea",' said the older boy suddenly, portentously, his empty pretty eyes full of meaning. Good lord. It seemed the entire family had now missed the point.

'How's the cider, son?' asked his father. 'Fine,' said Mart, acidly, with a look that said, you never call me son. The littler one, who had been playing with a handheld console of some sort throughout this exchange, was now kicking at the bar under the table, bored no doubt by a competition he couldn't begin to understand and was perhaps quite unaware of; kicked and kicked so that our drinks trembled as if at the approach of a beast. 'Stop that, Will,' hissed his mother.

I put my hand on my wife's knee, gave it a little squeeze. Take note, young Martin; take note Bob, or Jim or Bill or Barry, or indeed Alf or Fred as it may be; she is with me. She chose me.

Will, who had sulkily desisted, was now staring at us in a way that I felt might also warrant a reprimand. 'How old are you?' he asked. 'Will,' said Linda. 'That's not a question to ask a lady!' — with a simper that seemed a bid for sympathy. 'Why is your hair white?' he persisted, wilfully oblivious. My wife leaned across the table and confided: 'I'm a hundred and twenty-one,' and sat back, smiling. 'It's the sea air,' she said breezily. 'It does wonders for the complexion. You should have seen me a week ago. Richard here, for example, is well over six hundred years old.' We all laughed, awkwardly, unsure who was being made fun of; little Will went red and looked confused and went back to kicking the table, and Linda this time left him to it.

The hilarity subsided. I drained the last drop of whisky. I said, Well, we should be going. 'Gosh, yes!' she said, the first time I have ever heard her use this exclamation, looking at her wrist as if she wears a watch, a little pantomime all her own, as if there were some pressing engagement that we must attend to. Some submarine rendezvous perhaps. 'Oh, really? What a shame!' said Linda, not sorry at all. I helped my wife into her coat and wound her scarf around her neck and she kissed me, with the relief of departure, kissed me with her red mouth, the sharp sugary sour-ness of the sweets mingling with the bitter gin on her tongue.

'Well, maybe we'll see you around,' said Bob. Not if I see you first, I didn't say. I wonder if I should invest in a telescope. Mr Begg will surely have one in stock. As I held the door for her I saw the older boy give an unacknowledged wave, which became a self-conscious tug at the flop of his fringe; his father said something I didn't hear, and they all laughed, and Linda said 'Bill!' indulgently and they turned back to his camera, somehow reunited.

'I thought they seemed nice. A nice family,' she said, when we got home. Had those boys been on her mind all the way back, then? Did you think so? I said, dismissive. 'Well, they seem a normal family. Nicer than mine.' This was more interesting. A way in. Mine, too, I suppose, I said. Cautious; not wishing to push this confessional mood too far. I followed her to the fireside, bottle in hand. I thought of my parents, either side of their faux-marble fireplace, the gas turned high, all of us breathing the same air over and over. So much of my childhood was spent indoors, stifling; even when we went out we seemed insulated.

I imagine you an elfin child, I said, barefoot and ragged, running about with sand in your toes, with leaves in your hair. But, 'I was neat and clean,' she protested, accepting a glass and settling. 'My mother ironed everything. My clothes were starched into two dimensions. She ironed my school tie. She ironed my knickers. It made me feel guilty, to fill those clothes with substance. She'd be furious with me if I came home dirty or creased.' Poor girl; skin, hair, voice, all pressed flat. These days she is perpetually tangled. 'It wasn't her fault, really,' she said. 'She didn't expect a baby so late. She never got over having me. The milk turned sour inside her.' Like love, it curdled, and no amount of beating could smooth it back to cream. Her young skin, creamy and beaten, and bruised so easily. My precious girl.

Go on, I said gently, wary of breaking this spell of revelation; she has never given away so much.

'Sometimes,' she said, 'she'd stay in her room and not come out, and then I'd play in the garden, by the pond, I'd play with the frogs and the fish, with a bucket, in my pants and a vest, I'd make potions with pond water and petals and spit.' Little witch. Were you lonely? I asked. On your own like that, with only the frogs? 'I suppose I was. I didn't know any different. But I'd like to have had a brother. Or a sister. Would you?' she asked. 'I had books, instead of friends.' Myself, likewise, I said; and I was most glad of them, when I discovered how effective a barrier a book can be to unwanted acquaintance. Or, indeed, a retreat when acquaintance palls; how many women have been exasperated by this tactic? This, of course, I kept to myself.

'If I had been asked to choose, then, I would happily have never read another word, if I could have had a sister. I would be illiterate, for a sister,' she said, almost vehement. But without books, we would never have been lovers, I did not say. But you are my bookish and studious and brilliant wife; if you didn't read you would be none of those things. We would never have met. If there were no books, how could you have found me? Would you love me at all if it weren't for poetry, for stories? Do you take it so lightly, to be my wife? I said none of this. I said only: is that true? Illiterate? and tried not to sound horrified. She laughed. 'Well, maybe not. I don't know what use a sister would have been if I couldn't talk about books with her.' What a relief.

I pulled her close to my side, a warm, comforting, encouraging hug. Tell me more, I said. I want to know everything about you; tell me about your home, I urged, tell me about where you came from. She dismissed me as always: 'Oh, anywhere. Nowhere.' But tell me, I said, holding down her shrug with a hand on her shoulder. Tell me about that bright-haired girl, growing up in the cold north. 'In Morpeth,' she said. 'We moved to Morpeth, when I was a baby.' Yes, I said. What a name for a place. 'A path where a murder took place,' she said. 'That's where I lived. Once a man was murdered and they built a town to mark the spot.'

Tell me about that town, named for a forgotten crime, I pressed . . . She sighed. 'It's just a place,' she said. 'Unhaunted. Made of stone. Far from everywhere. Not far enough.' Unwilling to excavate that cold, unyielding home that she shared with her hard, unyielding mother. Another part of her buried in darkness. Far enough from what? I asked. She didn't answer.

Where, then, where is far enough? I asked. Here? Did you miss it? Did you want to come home, to your father's island? She shrugged. I don't know if she no longer cares to find him, or if she cares too much. She fell silent and looked through her glass into the fire, hugging her knees to herself; I couldn't read the sadness that I thought I saw, hollowing her eyes. In the classroom she was always bright, crystalline, apparently impervious; did I miss it, then, or is it coming to this place that has shivered something in her? Or perhaps it is just that, as she says, I am only now getting to know her; only now, here, seeing the shades and angles of her, cast into relief by the watery daylight and the soft dark.

In bed, now, her spine a long shadow lit by the faint moon, her lips a little parted; I kiss the splay of one webbed hand. She turns in her sleep and sighs, that heavy night-sigh like a last contented breath. The covers have slipped from her shoulder. I kiss the light on it and she pulls the blanket closer. All I can see of her skin is the barest pale crescent of her ear.

She turns, moans, sighs. Pulls the bedding about her in a cocoon. A body wrapped in a sail for a winding sheet.

She murmurs. I can't make out the words.

There is this extravagance to her always — she wanders beyond reach, beyond meaning. I trace the moon on her skin and cannot understand it. I turn it over, like the paperweight stone in my palm: why did we come here? Is this far enough?

Friday

She is wearing a particularly erratic outfit today, a baggy pair of linen trousers tucked into chunky socks and boots, a cable-knit sweater pulled in at the waist with a belt stolen from my cords, a silk scarf bunched at her neck and her green coat over it all. She does always wear green, and grey. It's true. Yet I can't quite shake the image of her in purple. Coming into my seminar room dressed in heather; or drenched . . . It's been a week, here, and already all else is receding. My little landlocked dark brown study seems another, smaller world, and I cannot imagine the heavy silence of the sea's absence, the thick heat, the dust. Everything is refigured in the air here. So now I am remembering her, in the sunlight last week in her silk, and the picture is diffused in this island's mist. I remember her sliding out of her silk on our wedding night, and think of her this morning at the mirror, pulling her gown over her head. Bleariness at the margins of sight; I am tired, not altogether unpleasantly.

All through the night she twisted and slithered, swimming about on the sheets without waking, without rest, and the night seemed to stretch for hours, and I listened to her murmur half-words and moan until the dawn. She rose early, stirring me from some kind of sleep; I felt her move away and made a grab for her but she stood up into a long stretch, escaping my grasp. She'd dreamed of being called into the water: 'there were arms, pale arms reaching for me,' she said, 'they pulled me under, down and under and out; way down into the dark.' She was looking at herself in the mirror, as if seeking evidence of a transformation; I watched through half-open eyes as she turned away, lifted her nightgown, hesitated, pulled it over her head, looking askance at herself with her shoulders turned inward as if trying to hide while she looked for clothes. Her long, pale arms protecting her body. What are you hiding from? I said. Just look at you. 'You look,' she said. She stepped out of her reflection and squared her shoulders to face me, blushing, defiant. Come here, come here, but stay so I can see you . . . We've been married a week, I told her. Term will be starting on Monday, without us. Can you believe it's a year since we met? Do you remember, last autumn? How you came into the room out of the wind, the rain . . . 'With leaves in my hair,' she smiled. Where on earth did you come from? I said. She didn't answer, but laughed, and climbed back onto the bed and crawled up the length of me. 'Happy anniversary, Professor,' she whispered, stretching out beside me, and pulling me down to her, into her dream.

I woke a few hours later and couldn't remember her leaving; only a slippery memory of her pale arms, reaching out to me; something watery, something shining, swum out of her sleep into mine. This morning as I look out to her and my mind blanks, I feel them again reaching.

She has her face turned towards the sun, where it trails and tingles the water. Listening for the wash of light. The air luminescent and she glowing with it. She seems at home here; she belongs. 'Take me north,' she said. And so it seems that my honeymoon is to be occupied by a series of seascapes with a woman at their centre: sometimes a girl, sometimes no more than a brightness quivering against the coming rain; or in the sudden northern sun, with a halo of white fire and her hair flaming; with her hair blown back; standing with her palms by her sides, turned out to feel the sea-mist borne in on the wind; with her chin resting on her clasped hands.

I want to retrieve and store every flake of skin that she chews from her lip and so carelessly spits out to the mercy of the wind. Yet when she is not right beside me, when I think of her in her absence, I am able to catch at only the smallest of scraps, as if a picture frame were placed about her elbow, the left one, with a freckle on the sharp bone; or the stab of her ankle and her long, spiny foot; or sometimes for an instant, the grey-green of her iris catching the sea's light; or the twin dips at the base of her back; or her crooked eye-tooth that gives her grin its glint; but all of these things seen only for a moment distinctly before vanishing, and if I try to reconstruct her from these known facts — her tooth is crooked, the freckle is just there, her eyes are sometimes green or sometimes grey or sometimes the nameless colour of clouds gathering or . . . well, the task is hopeless. I can only endeavour to keep her in view, and be assured of her presence for these moments at least. There she stands, bright, defiant, only just or almost manifest, between the sea and the sky. So I would have her remain, in just that pose; I close my eyes to fix her there.

When I open them she has already wandered off along the shore.

Those boys are with their father out on the cliffs, our cliffs, looking down on our bay. I recognize Bob's blue windcheater, his sons' lope and slouch, the silly baseball cap that the younger one wears and Martin's grotty parka. I can see them, passing binoculars and book between them, following the swoop of the gulls as they dive. As I look out, watching from the kitchen window while bashing prawny brains for tonight's fish stew, I see my wife pick her way over the rocks and seaweed, hair salt-frazzled, poking out in dry hanks from under her hat.

She surveys the horizon from the tide line, a bizarre pirate scoping the sea and the shore; seeing them above, she sweeps off her hat in an extravagant gesture so that, perhaps, they can't mistake her (as if they ever could), and waves it in the air. The older boy gives a half-wave back, binoculars trained on her, this rarest of species.

For a horrified moment there I thought they would descend, or worse, that she would climb up to them; but she glances back at the house, and she waves, in turn, at me in the window. She gestures for me to come out and join her, but I shake my head and brandish the brain-stained rolling pin, so she returns my shrug with a pout before pulling her hat back on, casting a last wave up to the cliff-top, and turning to walk the other way, along the shore. The boy still watching. I imagine her there in his glass, as if he were pressed up against her, breathing hot and urgent down her neck; the fibres of her hat, her hair swept round in the silk, the worn seams, the warm nape. That old hormonal jolt. Oh I remember that, Mart.

I smash at the pan.

When I look up, she has moved beyond the frame of the window, but he is still watching; she must be in his view, still.

Existing for him and not me.

I smash, smash.

*

At last, his father gave him a nudge and turned to go, and after a few reluctant seconds, he followed. I went back to my pan, although in truth the contents were thoroughly pulverised. A minute later I heard her come in, and stubbornly refused to answer her call, as if the prawns could spare none of my attention. I heard her drop her bag down by the door with a familiar clatter, like a set of bagpipes, the old worn leather and the wooden handles. That bag, I remember it from the seminar room; she'd come in with her haul of books, the thing was all corners, poking at the leather, stretching and yellowing. And she'd rummage about in the depths for a pen, pulling out notebooks and hankies and apples and paper-scraps, and one book after another stacked on the floor until at last she reached the object of her dig. All those books, scrawled all over, the narrow thread of her thoughts winding between the lines, filling the white space with ripples and eddies and waves. Her hand stained blue.

Now her bag sits there like a sad old emptied skin. She carries her pencil, her sketchpad, and whatever detritus she's gathered from the beach. The sand must be silting all through the lining, where it's torn.

She called; I didn't answer; smash, smash.

'Richard!'

She came in to the kitchen and kissed me on the cheek. Ah, you're back, I said, as if I hadn't heard her. 'I am,' she said. How is the sea today?

'That family were up on the cliffs, did you see?' she said. I grunted. Bird-watching, as leery old Bob would no doubt have it. 'What do you mean?' she said. I think you've revived the boy's interest in ornithology, that's all, I said, still desultorily fixated on the pan. At least in a certain silver-crowned sea bird. Or marine biology, that was his thing, wasn't it. He thinks he's spotted himself a mermaid.

I live in fear of holiday friendships, of having to invite our fellow travellers in for awkward cosy fireside chats. I have never been one for casual acquaintance. Why, simply because we find ourselves stranded together on this island, should we presume to form a community? Why should I have anything at all in common with a man who drinks his whisky 'on the rocks'? Well, he won't find any in this house. The best I could muster is a handful of pebbles. Or he's welcome to sit out there on them. Today I haven't got it in me to be gracious. I didn't sleep well.

'Well, they're leaving tomorrow anyway,' she said. Oh yes? I said. How do you know? 'They were down on the beach,' she said. When? I didn't see them. 'I don't know,' she said. 'Maybe you weren't looking. I assume you don't spend all your time just watching me.' Of course not, I muttered.

When was this? Can she not be left for a moment?

'I gave him my email address,' she said. 'He's thinking of applying to the old alma mater after all . . .' Don't they have an alumni network for that sort of thing? I snapped. 'I *am* an alum. Don't be such a curmudgeon,' she said. I harrumphed.

'I am an alum,' she said again, ignoring me, musing. 'Why does that word make me think of onions . . . ? Allium. I am an onion.' I refused to laugh or forgive her, but couldn't resist the game. No, I said, you are a budding flower; a pom-pom of blossom. 'Smelling of garlic,' she said. 'What's for dinner?'

Fish stew, I said, bashing, until she put a hand on my arm to stay it. 'I think they're dead now,' she said, peering into the bright orange mess of legs and burst beaded eyes and celery and shell.

So, this boy of yours, I asked. Will you write to him? 'Oh, I don't know,' she said, with a sigh of indifference, or impatience. 'He's not "mine".' Perhaps you could exchange poetry, I suggested. He seemed to have inherited his father's taste for it. In Xanadu . . . I intoned. 'Oh, don't be cruel,' she said. 'That poor man. He wanted to impress you.' I rather think he wanted to impress *you*, I said. She snorted, rolled her eyes, shook her head. And did he? I asked, trying not to sound pettish. Impress you, I mean. 'Richard,' she said. 'Really. What do you think?'

I stirred, needlessly, banged the spoon needlessly hard against the pan. I don't have your email address, I said pathetically. You've never given me your email address. Not your private one. (She always addressed me formally, 'Dear Professor _____, please find my essay attached,' and I would scour the screen for some other meaning, a hidden kiss; she signed off 'Yours . . .', not sincerely or faithfully, and I had to make do with that – simply mine.) 'Oh, poor Richard,' she said. 'Do you want it? You can have it, you know. You can send me emails from the next room. You can be working in the study and I'll be in the sitting room and you can write "Tea? Smiley face," that sort of thing.'

What does she mean to do there, lounging on the sofa while I work, I wonder? How will my muse amuse herself?

You're making fun of me, I said. And I don't do smiley faces. 'No,' she said. 'I've noticed. Not today, anyway.' And she put her thumbs to the corners of my mouth and pulled them up, as one inspects the gums of a dog.

Now the stew is eaten, the last of the juices mopped up with torn bread, staining our cuticles orange. As I cleared our plates and put them in the sink I asked, am I really a curmudgeon? She nudged me out of the way with her hip, turned on the tap, picked up the stained rolling pin and pointed it at me. 'You're *my* curmudgeon,' she said. 'Yes, I think that's what I shall call you. If I am your Ariel, your Vivien, your Melusine, etcetera, you can be my curmudgeon.' I said, I think I'd prefer . . . Prospero? Merlin? Some other old man at the end of his powers? Foolish, cursed Raymond? I think I'd prefer Richard, I said. 'Oh, very well,' she sighed. 'Richard it is.' And I stowed the last plate in the rack to dry, and made for the sitting room. 'If you're going to be cur-mudgeonly about it,' she said, behind my back. When I turned reproachfully, she seemed absorbed in sponging the cutlery clean, all innocent, as if she hadn't spoken. Her teasing, I suppose, will keep me young. I live in hope.

'Did you miss me this afternoon, Richard?' she said, following me a few minutes later and finding me sulking quietly on the rug, staring into the fire. She put two glasses down on the hearthstone, and pulled me back to rest my head on her knees. 'Is that all it is? I've come back, see? I'm all yours.' Do you promise? I asked, as she circled my temples; 'all mine? You'll stay with me?' and she bent her face over so her hair fell on my chest and my head was enclosed in the cave of her curved body, the smell of the sea on her, a thick dark salt heat, she kissed me and I took it for her answer gladly.

We sat in the fire's glow. I scribbled at my notebook and she sketched, with her new pad and pencil. I didn't know she liked to draw. She says she hasn't 'for ages, not since school'. The compression of her 'ages'. Like the difference between history and geology. Her youth as recent as the turn of the last century, and mine long since become a fossil. Well. I scribbled and sipped my drink and she sketched, her gaze intent; every now and again I'd glance up and she'd smile and then frown, because I had disturbed her composition – but first she smiled, as if she cannot help but smile when she meets my eye. Silent, but for the sound of our hands on the paper, little incremental shuffles in the struggle to make record. As couples spent evenings of old.

She was very still, only her shadowed eyes flickering and the curve and dart of her left hand. The firelight cast her cheekbones, her wide pale brow, the line of her Grecian nose, the point of her chin in high relief; the deep hollows of her eyes and cheeks; a momentary portrait, an exercise in chiaroscuro. If I had canvas and oils, a palette of red, umber, gold, for the pale flame of her hair lit by the embers, a dab of ochre and white for the dip of her cupid's bow; if I had an artist's cap, an artist's eye; if I had world enough and time I would have made of this an endless sitting. But tonight, I was her subject.

'There he sits,' I imagine her thinking. 'My husband, wise and kind and vigorous, with his dark eyes hooded, his brow just so' – her pencil flicks over the page – 'the scrape of his chin which juts just a little; his hair, which is wiry, become jagged where he has wiped his brow with his forearm, sweating over the stove, so that it stands in a comical coif. Shall I mock him? Has he had enough teasing? Or shall I smooth it softly and kiss him, and call him my curmudgeon, tenderly?'

But she did neither, just went on sketching intently, and flicking her eyes over my hairline and back to the page. And perhaps she was recalling her suave and sleeked Professor of three terms hence, and perhaps she was merely thinking, 'Who is this unkempt old man? Must he slurp his wine so?'

No, it may not be long before the morning when she, watching me over breakfast, thinks 'who is this absent-minded, woolly old man, with jam on his sleeve' – I cannot deny it – 'pushing his specs up his nose, pursing his lips?' Will she come to despise these breakfast-time gestures as ardently as I adore hers? Will she dread each night, sitting up reading, her husband peering at the page beside her, longing for a touch but not his? The sight failing, the body failing. What will go first? Heart, liver, lungs? How many years from now? She in the fullness of her fertility, tucking a blanket to swaddle her incontinent husband. And when it comes to it, she will be a lovely widow, she will be lovely still. Oh, it is unfair, it is unjust — that there she will stand, by the graveside, grieving, still existing when I am gone and cannot watch her, and some boy on the edge of the graveyard can.

But no, she showed me her work, and she has made me handsome, savage and dark; it seems I glower as I read. It is a good likeness; or a pleasing likeness, at least. Which, for the vainglorious sitter, amounts to the same thing.

Saturday

I woke this morning to her calling me from the bathroom, 'Richard?' I was half-asleep still, drowsy; her voice distant, so that I couldn't be sure I'd heard her. Some siren calling me out of a dream, from a far shore. I struggled upwards. Again, 'Riii-chaard,' I heard her, calling across the water; then sharply: 'Richard!' and I woke. Impatient imp.

I rose, and found the door to the bathroom ajar, and went into the sweet-salt steam of her lair; she was in the tub, full almost to brimming, chin-deep in honey-scented bubbles, smiling shyly. And then she sat forward, and raised a smooth leg pink from the water and soaped it, and as ever I felt the shock of her woman's body, which spends its days in such formless garb that I forget, under the men's shirts and shapeless nightgowns and knitwear is this long, muscular, shapely form, marmoreal. The sheen on her shin, her long feet. My Melusine rising from the water.

'There you are,' she said. 'Did I wake you? Richard,' she announced, 'I must learn to swim.' Must you? I said. I hope you're not planning to make your leap any time soon, my little water snake. Not in that sea, I said. It's perishing.

'I mean it, Richard. Don't make fun of me. You have to help me. I'm scared of the water, I can't go under. Will you hold me under?' And she took my wrists then, quite suddenly and with a surprising grip, and placed my palms on her shoulders and looked at me, beseeching, with those great eddying eyes of hers. My darling, I said, hold you under? I was unnerved, ready to laugh, seeing she was serious. 'Please,' she said, 'I can't do it alone. You must. I've been trying, I've been trying half an hour now and I can't force myself under.' And it was true, her hair was stuck a little to her dewed forehead, it hung in wet hanks and clung to her shoulders and her breasts, but the crown was quite dry.

She took a great deep breath and pinched her nostrils and her eyes widened, huge, before she squeezed them shut, and I felt her tense under my hands, and so help me, if only to break that tension I pushed her under, forced those bony shoulders under before I knew what I did. And as soon as she was under her eyes flew open again, I watched her face through a frame of bubbles, and her body bucked, but her grip on my right wrist stayed firm so that she almost held herself there, with my hands. And feeling her flesh tremble, and seeing her young body twist with the torsion of an electric eel, and meeting those wide and scared sea-green eyes, I felt my blood rise for her then; so strong her grip and her frame so narrow.

And then, she went rigid and still, and even when I no longer held her, she stayed under, would not relinquish my wrist, and it seemed hours I spent there, watching her, in her grasp, wanting her, fearing her a little, until at last I could stand it no longer, I broke before she did and hauled her up, I gripped her shoulders harder and pulled her back into the world, and I think if I hadn't she might have stayed there. And she gasped, as if waking, struggling for air; she gasped and laughed and kissed my palms and thanked me. 'I'm fine! I'm still alive!' she cried. Only just, I said. How long did you plan to stay down there? 'I didn't feel like I needed air at all!' she gasped. But you do, you do, you must remember to keep breathing, you must come up for air, I said. And I kissed her, her wet lips, and she pulled me down, pulled me into her, underwater.

She looks back now from the beach and sees me with my books and thinks I am gainfully employed, still wrestling mermaids. But all I can think of is her eyes under the water, her hands on my wrists; and the squeak of elbows and knees against the sides of the bath, and the bruise surely forming at the top of her spine where it pressed into the enamel, and her chin bruising the tendon of my shoulder; I am a mass of distraction, anxiety, desire. How could I have held her under so easily? Her euphoria, dizzied, oxygen-starved, infecting me; her body pinned in my hands and yet escaping me, impossible to pin down. What is it she's afraid of, that she would go to these lengths? When I ask, she says, 'Of drowning.' As if it were obvious. Last night she dreamed a new nightmare, of a shipwreck; she was trapped in it, she found a man drowned and she couldn't get away, she said. She couldn't tell me more but sat up in the dark, shivering, unwilling to go back to sleep; feeling herself on the threshold, the sea waiting to swallow her again. I stroked her back, fought to stay awake and soothe her, I held her, hushed her, until, exhausted, she consented to lie back down and I whispered you won't drown, who drowned? But if she answered I was already sleeping.

When she told me she dreamed of the sea I had imagined some benign subconscious realm; is it only proximity that has raised the monsters from the bed? And why, again why, then, have we come here? Or perhaps, all the while, when she sat in my seminars, in my office, in my garden, as we lay together in the sunshine, on the grass – perhaps she was haunted all the time by it. Did she go into that darkness every night when we were parted? I try to recall a sign, some shadow around the eyes, and cannot, or think I can, but can't quite place it; a shadow or a flash of silver.

Mermaids and water nymphs; all those tearless, tongueless, soulless creatures, their mysterious submerged lives . . . I look back to my books and still, all I can see is her eyes under the water, her eyes full of the sea.

Out on the shore now, she bends to retrieve some shard or shell that will no doubt be added to the collection on the table; she has made a sort of cairn, a small burial mound of sea-relics, a memorial to some tiny, lost thing. She leaves little in the way of traces, apart from these shells, pebbles, drifts of sand; an occasional bright hair trailing. Each day she brings her offering, not knowing how precious is the privilege of merely having her return, be it empty-handed or bearing gifts. They are warm on the sill as I sort through them, disturbing the arrangement of a spell, perhaps.

Her latest finding: A fragment of bone, from a sheep I'd guess from the scale. It is a rusted grey, sea-smoothed to stone, but hollow and porous and rough to the touch within like ossified sponge. Long since stripped of blood and marrow and life. Except that one might imagine, in those tiny hidden holes, a riddle of worms writhing, or tiny insects, picking it clean.

I pick up the bone and watch her through it, like a primitive, useless telescope. It makes the brightness brighter, enamelled; it arrests her there for a moment. And then she moves beyond it, suddenly gone from the circle.

*

Last night's terrors and this morning's strange antics have been
smoothed away by her unwillingness to acknowledge them as
such. It seems a dream now, or a game, which should be easily
forgotten. I was chary of her over breakfast until she asked, 'Is
something wrong?' with such innocent concern, as if she couldn't
think what might be, that I said I was preoccupied with work and
wanted to just pin something down; a lie, and a regrettable choice
of phrase but she didn't register it. She simply left me to it. So I
went back to my books and my watery women, then, for the sake
of appearances. Undine; poor Undine. The knight Hildebrand
or Huldbrand falls in love with the water nymph's wayward,
elemental beauty. Girlish, giggling, and then suddenly wilful;
younger than her years, naïve; and then again knowing, and
unknown, and utterly remote. She marries him, and gains a soul;
exchanging immortality, willingly, for love. Eventually, inevitably, she is betrayed, and resolves again into water . . . Will I tell
her this one, I wondered? Would she like it? Perhaps not.

Every line I write now is written to fit her, and none will
suffice.

After a couple of hours of this desultory note-making and restless
observation, I gave up and went out to her. I stood behind her and

pressed my warmed hands to her neck, lifting her hair to look for the tender circle of purple that sure enough I found below her nape. I felt an odd, half-familiar twist in my gut as I recalled her hands on my wrists and our limbs squashed together in the water, her body crushed under me; how ready I was to submit to her, to this strange impulse in her. I brushed the bruise gently with my thumb. She made a little moaning sigh. I asked if she was all right. 'I'm fine,' she said, as if there was no reason for my asking. 'What are you up to?'

I thought I might go for a walk, I said, feeling somehow that I ought to excuse my presence on her beach. Want to come? She looked pleased, I think. She wound her chilly fingers through mine. I bought her gloves but she doesn't wear them. I chafed her hands; thin, knuckly, green-veined and perished with cold. Her bitten nails. The base of her thumb is a shining knobble of bone, almost arthritic.

'Let's go,' she said, despite the low grey sky, blurring into the rough-hewn marble of the dark sea.

As we climbed up from the cottage to the main path we came in view of a stolid old soul, cable-knit and capable, plodding along in wellington boots. He paused at a gate in the fence and turned to watch us ascend, glancing over my open but hopelessly stiff shirt collar, my old cords, my impractical shoes, flat and soft-soled leather, perfect for padding the labyrinths of academe but quite useless out here in this treacherous terrain; he soon had the measure of me and let his eyes slide to rest instead, inevitably, on her. Hair plaited and hatted, she looked her age even at a distance; despite the sweaters and scarves that as ever overwhelmed her, she gambolled and twirled, girlish, turning to encourage me to clamber on. We reached the top of the path and looked out to sea, standing beside him; I took a theatrical, chest-slapping, much-needed gulp of air. For something to say, which seemed required, I noted that the sun was coming out – just as it began to creep beneath the clouds again.

'Aye,' he said.

Neither party moved off. I had no intention of gaining a companion on this constitutional, but had still to catch my breath. So we stood there together, looking out at the sea.

'Aye, hid's kinda changey the day,' he said eventually. 'Whar is it thee're stayin'?'

That's us just down there, I said.

'Oh, aye, the noust hoose,' he said. 'Just theesael, is it?' he said, squinting slyly at me. Unless it was only the sunshine.

Yes, just myself, and my wife, I said.

'Oh, aye,' he said, and fell silent, and she said nothing and watched the sea and ignored his sidelong stare, if she was aware of it. Well, we'd best be getting on, I said, and he nodded and grunted and I put an arm around her shoulder, and she kept looking out, turning her head as I turned her body to the path as if she were a covetous child and I dragging her from the object of her craving; or as if leading her from a horror she couldn't tear her eyes from.

I've been meaning to ask, I said – Noust hoose? So our cottage seems to be known, although I've seen no signs to say so. 'A noust is a docking place, a boat shelter,' she explained. 'A hoose is a house, Richard,' except she said 'hyce', like the Queen, as if for my benefit. 'A dwelling-place. A residence.' A gentleman's home is his castle, I said humbly.

We reached a cattle grid where the road dipped and as she picked her way daintily across it, lifting her skirts like a lady crossing a puddle, I looked back and saw him, still on the crest of the rise, still watching. Then when I next looked back, he was gone.

We made our way back down to the sea by the slabby black rocks that enclose each sandy bay; trying to pick a path across the dry places, and the runnels of sand between – the rock is slick like oil and more than once I felt a sickening slip under my sole before righting myself. The flats and crevices between the ridges are strewn with snake-like seaweed, thick, whitish and rust-red fleshy ropes, with a bunching of flat maroon fronds at the head. A massive slew of it, piled up on the white sand, slimed with red and orange like a giant's plate of giant spaghetti; 'or like entrails,' she said. 'Like some massive thing was gutted here and the innards left to rot.' A gift for the macabre, she has. My charming wife.

A little way along the shore, climbing up again to the grassy links that edge it, we came upon a half-ruined house, just like our own cottage in the next bay, built in the same low, layered grey stone, but derelict. Such dwellings are everywhere on the island, in varying states of disrepair; there is no call to demolish them, I suppose, when space is hardly at a premium. Some with only the gable ends to show the shape of the pointed roof that has long since collapsed, the interior long since grassed over, deserted for years by all but the rabbits. They might have been abandoned twenty or two hundred years ago, the landscape closing back in around them. The last of a succession of civilisations to leave their remnants. The Vikings, the Picts, the Norwegians, Christians and heathens have left their stones, too, behind them. The floor of the old church where we renewed our vows. Beds hewn into the walls of houses. She says there is an ancient settlement on the Mainland that lay buried until a storm tore the earth from it, five thousand years after it was abandoned by whoever lived there. And no one knows who they were or what became of them. Round brochs and cairns and burial mounds; old worship, old defences, long-forgotten tombs. Their builders long departed, their bones long laid to rest. What we leave behind us. How solid, the shell of life remaining.

There were trees, once, on these islands; when they were all cut down, she says, there were none to replace them. And then it grew cold; the people struggled, where once they had prospered; there were centuries of hardship, and they clung on, men such as I imagine her father, strong, tall, grim men from the north, with their coarse hardy crops and their thick-woolled flocks, they held on, and they died or passed through, and others came, and only the stones remained.

In the cemetery, there are ranks and ranks of the same few families' graves; children and babies and husbands and wives, the old folk and the taken, the departed Beggs and Odies and Donaldsons. Some worn to a wafer of stone, the slate flaking and bent; the graves like cliff-top markers, facing the sea, the names worn away by the wind, worn to silence. That day we reaffirmed our vows, we walked there; now I think of how she walked up and down, peering at each in turn, as if seeking a trace of herself. Running her fingers over them, feeling for a message in the stone. But it was only the same names, over and over, and none of them the one that she has lately relinquished.

All of these, besides, long dead, none buried here for a century past, the worshippers long departed to the lowly pebble-dashed building along the road from here. All these lives, ended before modernity, such as it is, ever reached this island; all lived by gaslight and warmed by the peat, and coming to rest at last looking out to sea, to the sea that perhaps returned them lifeless. 'How many drowned?' she said. 'Look: these men. Only thirty, only twenty-eight, only eighteen. Only twenty-one. I wonder how many drowned.'

Only twenty-one. Can she have any notion what that means? I am unsettled by the darkness, I think, closing in, and the strange day of ill, changing light; I sit alone in silence by the fire, which seems a lonely comfort, a scant human crackle of flame against the rush of wind and the sea.

This particular ruin on the beach, in fact, was still roofed; and, peering in, it would seem not so very long abandoned. It is easier, somehow, to accommodate those houses long left to the elements, already absorbed into a dateless past. But whoever left this house seemed to have done so only lately, and quite suddenly. Set down his cup of tea on the table, stood, went to the door, closed it behind him and said no, I shan't come back. Left the dishcloth to stiffen by the sink; left the furniture to swell and moulder in the damp. Steel taps that look like they might still turn; tattered curtains at the cracked window. The scraps left hanging were sun-yellowed, printed with a big, brown and yellow sunflower design on a thick-woven synthetic cloth.

'These remind me of my childhood,' she said. 'Everything brown and yellow and green and orange, with prints like this. The last of the seventies, left over. The carpets and the curtains and the cushions and my mum's dresses, everything.' I passed no comment. I, too, remember these patterns, these colours; I remember when women like her mother wore dresses made of cloth like those curtains, swinging above the knee. I remember the scratchy thick metal zips at the back, I remember unzipping them. Red wine and Rimbaud . . . This past I have no use for, since she can have no part there.

We circled to look into the bedroom: an iron bedstead in the centre of the room stood crooked and unused, without a mattress; but in the corner, a blanket, a sleeping bag. A pillow, perhaps a little mildewed, but somehow I thought it might be warm to the touch, just in the centre where a head had left an indent. An empty can of Tennent's, bent in two, the logo unfaded. A newspaper; I couldn't make out the date or the headline, but it was unyellowed, the masthead still tabloid-red. 'Someone lives here,' she whispered. Detritus piled up against the peeling, damp-stained walls – litter and driftwood. A pile of sardine tins. I had a momentary vision of a slobbering, monstrous ogre, staring crazed eyes, clasping its dinner in both hands; some grotesque giant shovelling the silver bodies into its mouth in oily handfuls.

'Shall we go in?' she said: eager, wide-eyed, quite, quite mad. Of course not, I said. I tried to laugh and found I could not. Dread suddenly all over me like cold fish scales, scraping and bristling. Let's go. They might come back, I said. Let's go. She looked at me, puzzled by my agitation. She peered in for a minute longer, cupping her hand against the glass, then turned back to me curiously and asked if I was all right. I'm fine, I said. Let's go. I led her away. It occurred to me that, aside from her horror of the sea, she is quite fearless; and I felt craven beside her, a timorous creature clutching onto her hand.

She was quiet as we walked home. Her fingers cold and nerveless, as if they might at any moment slip free. The sea-mist was thickening, it was getting dark, and cold with the dampness; the masked sun was already setting, casting a squeamish, greenish light through the pewtery clouds. I feared who we might pass, not wanting to stop, wanting to get her home. I could not dispel the sense that we were followed; by what? By that harmless old man, by the sardine-eating ogre, by the cemetery's spectres? But we saw no one. As the night draws in, the islanders keep to their cottages, I suppose. Still I find myself sitting up, now, and wondering, who might have been hiding, in the mist, in the dark. And at her eagerness to find out.

She is calling me.

Perhaps one last short measure. Perhaps I'll let her need me a little longer. One last dram and I'll take the bottle to her.

Sunday

An overcast, lowering sky this morning; the clouds have clotted through the night. Something gathering, brooding, out on the sea. A darkness spreading. The edges of my wife blur against the sky.

I stand at the window, sipping my tepid, burnt, weak brew in my striped pyjama bottoms and dressing-gown. I am quite grey in the mornings before coffee, and I am glad of her kindness – even though she doesn't drink it, and makes it dreadfully, scorching the grounds. I need it this morning especially. My head aches. I brought it on myself, pressing whisky on her and sousing myself in the process.

Mrs Odie has at last departed. Her knocking woke us; I had been dreaming, I think, of a ship, sailing on the troubled sea that haunts her. The house became a tiny cabin, buffeted from all sides, a terrible beating against the oak as if heavy tentacles would batter it down. I woke trapped in a tartan tangle to a banging at the door, the beast breaching the barrier; but it was only knocking, a polite knock, amplified by the shock of waking and the subsequent hangover flooding in with the light. Beside me, my wife had pulled the covers over her head, groaning, and was shoving at me gently to get up. I heard the key turn in the lock, threw on my robe and made, I thought, a magisterial entrance to the living room, crying Good morning, Mrs Odie! 'Oh, ah thought thee were oot,' she said, 'excuse me,' not in the least discomfited or stirred by the sight of my grey-furred chest. Not at all, Mrs Odie, carry on, I said grandly, delirious I think with fatigue. Mrs Odie carried on, taking up her basket and mop, tutting.

By the time I'd washed and dressed, my wife had dragged herself out of bed. I heard them talking in the kitchen; I feared remonstrance for the mess, and moved closer to listen, to step in and defend her if necessary. But to my surprise, it seemed to me a friendly exchange. I couldn't make out the words, but the tone was warm, the quick trill of my wife when she is being sociable, the soft rumble of Mrs Odie's consonantal roll . . . a murmur, a mumble, how sudden the weather changes, some cheerful premonition of doom, it sounded like. Something about whisky. 'Oh, we take just a glass before bed, Mrs Odie!' said my wife with a tinkly fairy-laugh that made an absurdity of the incontrovertible evidence, the bottles accumulating, the dried-brown stains in every glass, my own ragged visage. A laugh to obliterate reality.

I thought I heard her say her own surname, her maiden name.

Her father's name. And I recalled how in the night, I thought I heard her say, 'he drowned'.

Tell me about him, I asked again, late last night as we sat propped in bed. I poured more whisky and waited; I approached very delicately, very gently.

'I don't know,' she said eventually, after a long, dark silence; 'I was little when he left. He's gone. He sailed away,' she said vaguely, with a gesture out to sea; a rebuttal. We have circled these waters before now. I know, I said. I'm sorry. Tell me about him.

I topped up her glass; and as she loosened and langoured, I prised at her, my clamped little clamshell. I was gentle and generous with every measure, soothing with whispers and spirits. I told stories, circuitous, leading her back. The Forsaken Merman, left alone with his children, all of them pining, down and away below. Melusine's father, the Scots King Elynus.

Melusine, the daughter of the fairy Pressyne, is raised by her mother on the Isle of Avalon – Elynus is banished for breaking a promise, as they always do in these tales. Once grown, Melusine seeks him out and avenges this betrayal by sealing him in a cave in Northumbria. Whatever became of him, that poor Scotsman now confined to her unshared memories, walled up from the world? Strange, the forms she takes, or that will fit her. Flickering across her as she stands out there at the water – a glint of scale, a glimpse of silver. Did she stand with her father beside her once on that shore? Did he, one day, swim out and never come back? Could this be the sea her father sailed on, the sea that swallowed him under? Because of his absence, she does not like to speak of him; I think she fears she will betray him, with anger or grief or guilt. So I must be delicate and indirect. I fed out these morsels of stories, I hinted and prompted, but she wouldn't take the bait. I was patient.

At last she said, 'He was tall.' Like you, I said.

'Like me.' She smiled. A further silence.

Yes, tall, and? What else? She sighed, very quietly, almost contented. Her green eyelids heavy. I saw her eyes cloud over, and I had to lean in to hear her. 'He was huge. When I was little. Tall and broad and strong. He lifted me and I felt like Thumbelina, sitting in the palm of his hand.' Broad, strong, beloved. Vanished.

I topped up her glass.

'He delivered me, apparently. So the story goes. There was a storm, and we couldn't get to the Mainland. From wherever we were.'

Her grey eyes when they first opened looked on his face, turned topsy-turvy; he was the first to ever hold her. 'He used to read to me,' she said. 'I can't really remember. I had a little box bed and he'd have to duck to sit on the side of it. I remember it was always dark; the wind and the sea outside. Before we moved. But I was just a baby, so maybe I can't remember that. It must have been light sometimes.' We were, ourselves, still sitting up in bed, well wrapped against the night, the blind drawn against it; close, but not quite touching. I didn't dare disturb her. He taught her to speak, she said. In a low murmur that would not intrude upon her mother's fragile silence, he whispered words until she learned them, his islander's lilt, a sound like the sea. First, she says, Dada. I didn't go so far as to suggest that her father, who abandoned her so callously, was perhaps a rampant egotist, to teach her this above all.

'I needed to know how to get his attention,' she explained, simply. Didn't your mother mind, that it was never her you called for? 'Oh, no,' she said. 'I learned that was a bad idea before I even had words for it. No, I always called for him. And very quietly. I was a very quiet child.' Of course, of course she was. Quiet in a corner, twisting her white hair, calling to him when she had to, quietly. Until, one night, when she called for him, he was gone. And ever since – she does not say so but I see it – there has been that ache of absence, never dulled. She doesn't say how old she was when he went, or what she remembers of his departure; she offers nothing concrete. Too young perhaps to make any sense of it, old enough only to feel the loss. It is a kind of myth, her memory of him, right up to his mysterious vanishing.

Have you forgiven him? I asked. Such a look she gave me, then; everything suddenly sharp, her eyes narrowed like an angered cat's. 'I didn't need to forgive him. I loved him.' And then she drained her glass and when she held it out to me for refilling, she had somehow performed that little spell she has, spun a glamour about herself that is too bright to see past, so that she looked as though she'd never lost anything in her life. As I poured she lay back against the pillows and said, 'Are we done for today, Sigmund?'

I hardly slept at all, I drifted through the night half-sleeping, half-dreaming in a drunken reel, turning over and over again what she'd told me; as dawn came I was jerked by a sick lurch as she floundered and flailed and woke. 'He drowned, he drowned,' I thought she said, or else I dreamed it; I can't remember, she told me her dream or she said it in her sleep or I heard her say it, in mine. I reached for her out of my sleep, shook her gently and held her trembling; I raised her up and she surfaced, clinging, soaked through again with cold water. I kissed her face and tasted her sweat or tears or the sea. And I kissed her hands, her fingers, I kissed the damp membrane between them, tenderly; and she grasped my face then, and lifted it to meet hers and held me, transfixed, with her wild eyes; and she pulled her gown over her head, and I bent to kiss her again, seeking out the savour of desire in armpit and elbow and the hollows behind her knees, and she writhed and sighed and wrapped her limbs about me to trap my tongue where she wanted it, until the last salt surge exhausted her. And I lay with my head on her belly and listened to the murmur of her dream like the tide, until I too went under.

Over breakfast she was a little distant, lapsing into submerged silence as she pulled her toast to bits. She pressed crumbs into her plate with her fingers. She yawned, covering her whole face with a cave of hands; then rubbed her eyebrows and pulled them taut and sat with her head hanging from her hair in her fists. I asked if she'd slept badly. 'Mmm,' she said, getting up to boil the kettle. 'Oh no, did I wake you again?' I don't mind, I said. I'm getting used to it. She looked rueful. It has its advantages, anyway, I said — as long as you don't mind my keeping you awake a little longer. 'I can hardly object to that, can I?' she said.

Were you dreaming? I began, and she interrupted with a groan, leaning against the counter. 'Ugh . . . Hangover,' she said, accusatory. 'Mrs Odie thinks I'm a lush.' Oh dear, I said; I thought you seemed to be getting on rather well with her. What were you talking about? Apart from my bad influence, obviously? 'Nothing much,' she said. She said they were talking about the weather, she was just being polite. 'She thinks there's a storm coming. She says there's "a skuther blowan on the beach".' She cast a glance out of the window. I see, I said. I thought I heard you mention your father, I said casually, were you thinking she might know him? Carefully, carefully I prised at the chink where I'd felt her give way, a little, last night; but sober, she has closed herself up again. I have seen only the barest glimpse, a throb in the dark hollow of her shell. 'Why would I talk to a complete stranger about my dad?' she asked, not quite annoyed, but sharp enough to spike me. I must have misheard, I said. 'No one here would know him,' she said. 'I hardly even knew him.' I persisted, I just thought you said . . . 'Please, Richard,' she said then, and suddenly she looked exhausted, fraught, 'he went away. Let it go.'

She doesn't remember waking, for all my efforts to console her; and now I cannot say if I heard what I thought I heard, or if I dreamed it myself, her saying this, or if, possibly, in her confusion, her bewilderment, still drunk in the sodden aftermath of her nightmare, she let slip the truth.

Now she has gone out, to clear her head she says. The grey-green opaque light makes me uneasy. That, and her absence. The empty room behind me. The wind in the grate.

I am supposed to be working. My concentration wanes with every passing day, every troubled night. These paper-thin creatures on the page fail to fascinate as she does, although she is hardly more substantial.

I find I cannot look away, loath to leave her to the mercy of such a, such a skuther. I am assuming that this lovely word refers to the gusting, hectic, restless winds which have swarmed out of the greyness and are now lifting that silver hair up like a pale flame flickering. And she doesn't waver although it looks like she might at any moment be lifted and whirled out to sea; she stands her ground, watching. She says there were once women on these islands who could tell a storm coming; who could ride a boat in any weather, who would put out to sea to rescue the sailors they knew would be otherwise doomed, and these women, these storm-witches, were sometimes accused of bringing the storm, of calling it up, and were often hanged for their trouble. I see her fingers twitch.

Out at the sea's edge, the water churns over, a static rolling like horses pawing the ground; it comes to her feet in a wash of foam and fret. She is a kind of orphan, a ragged orphan, out there on the beach, as if abandoned. Wilfully abandoned. The forsaken mermen remain in their chariots, observing their daughter, with-holding, squinting into the strange glare.

A darkness out on the water, and over the cliffs. In years gone by, she tells me, men hid in those caves, evading the pressgangs of King George's navy. Gaping hollow sockets full of eyes in the darkness. The island to the west has smeared into the sea again.

The height of those waves, now. The wind scatters the sky, growing steadily stronger; it whips a stream up the cliffs in a spray, a plume like smoke, and her hair streaming upwards like that blown-back fall, too, like a fountain.

I'm heart-sore for wanting her, all the warm hollows of her, all the secret parts I would seek out. Her dreams, all washed through with seawater. Salt in the corners. Crumbs in the bed. Soaked, the sheets. Under the sheeny black surface, the currents that would whirl her down to the deep in her sleep, down to the giant squid and tentacles and stinging things and teeth and tendrils, and only the electric fish-lights to see by, down to the terror that reaches into her from the bottom of that ocean; the dark surface that sometimes glasses her eyes.

I am restless, fretful; unnerved by something, some echo I can't catch, a word that eludes me, a trail of brightness at the corner of my eye . . . Something I've forgotten.

'Let it go,' she said. I will have to get used to this, leaving her alone, when I return to work. Let her be; look away from the window, look to your books.

To work, for god's sake.

The knight-at-arms is left to loiter palely on the cold hillside by his Belle Dame. But in what sense is she without mercy? Because she shows him a world that he cannot inhabit, where she cannot keep him? Wraps him in fantasy and then abandons him to waste and rot? Or simply because she makes him love her, and then leaves? What is the nature of this enchantment? Or is it only madness, or a dream, and if so, whose?

Whose?

This is hopeless.

The sky is closed. No sign of the sun. The house is cold, the blankets damp, it's too dim to read, really. No; I won't let it go. I am unwilling to let her alone, this afternoon. How can I hope to get used to it? I will go out to her. Out on the beach, she

she is gone.

She can't have gone far. There isn't far to go. I keep checking to see if she will emerge from the sky, but no. There is no one else out there, on the cliffs, on the beach.

Her phone is switched off, or else out of range – nothing unusual in these parts. The seagulls scream, invisible. No birds sing. I shall wait another ten minutes and then go out to find her.

The same page in front of me still unread. Put it aside. It is too dim to read, really, anyway. Jacket, scarf; ignore the tremor, bundle it into my gloves. A withdrawal symptom, merely. A palsied liver, maybe, but a steady, a faithful, a loyal heart.

*

I went down to the beach and stood foot-deep in the squidgy brown kelp, looking from one edge of the bay to the other. No sign of her on the high cliffs, nor on the rocks. I have grown so accustomed to her standing just there that the space she ought to have occupied seemed crudely painted in, as if she'd been excised from the canvas and the hole hurriedly pasted. Where had she gone? Surely not far.

I found her footprints but they had been sucked away where they met the edge of the wet sand. I stood at the point of their vanishing and looked out; no sign of her, the sea at ebb, dissolving. I ran along the tide line, first one way, then the other, fighting the pull of the sand, not knowing which way to turn or where to look and beginning to panic, and then saw the track emerge again just a few metres off. As if she had walked up from the seabed in her boots, a modern-day Venus borne in on the foam. Then they stopped at the rocks; I could see nothing beyond the ridge. So I climbed after her. I skidded and slipped in my foolish shoes; every step could have splintered a bone. So preoccupied was I with my own precarious progress, placing one foot and then another in spite of the quake in my knees, that it was only when I reached the safe shore of the next bay, only when I had eased myself down onto the sand and rested with a hand propping my weight against the stone, breathing hoarsely, only when I looked up did I see her, standing further up the beach, talking to a stranger at the edge of visibility. She had her back half-turned to me; she hadn't seen me, and I in turn could not make out her face. He was a crooked figure, with a stick, a dirty blue cap covering his grimy hair; an old sailor, black grease bedded in his wrinkles, toothless, agape.

It may be that I have embellished this particular grotesque. And yet I see him still, clawing at her with a knotted hand. They parted after a minute or two; but who could say how long they had stood together thus before I saw them, their heads bent together, conspiring? Who knows what tricks he had up his filthy sleeve? Smiling his horrible hole of a smile at the peedie lass with her bonny bright locks? Sick, am I sick of a jealous dread? Can it be that I envy that old man, that ancient man, that old sea-troll? Cramming his toothless face with sardines?

For it was he, surely, the sardine-eater; off he went, then, to his hovel – looking back at her, surreptitious, to check that she was looking out to sea, and then making his spindly way up the links to the house we'd thought abandoned, back to his mildew and grog, the old sot.

'Richard?' she said, quite suddenly beside me. I had neither seen nor heard her coming. 'What are you doing here? Are you all right?' I came to find you, I said, lamely. With a weak gesture I said, Look at the sun setting, as if that was why I'd sought her out. And the sun obliged my lie, flooding the sea with oxblood, an angry red gash between the dark water and the low cloud.

'I didn't mean to worry you,' she said, undeceived. I just wondered where you'd gone, I said. I came to find you, I said again. 'I wasn't far,' she said. She carried a flail of seaweed, one of those that mass in the cracks of the rocks, as if it were a lash with which to whip a Caliban.

Who was that gentleman? I asked. 'Which one?' she said. How many have there been? Just now, I said, the older gentleman. Meaning, older than me. 'Oh, him. Poor old thing. He asked the time. I don't know that I'd call him a gentleman.' Oh no? I said. I am duty-bound to defend your honour if it has been compromised. 'No, I just mean, I shouldn't think he's gentry. Just a man.' You don't own a watch, I said. 'That's what I told him.' I said nothing. It seemed to me it had taken a long time for her to impart this information. 'I think he just wanted someone to talk to.' I think he's our sardine-feaster, I said. 'I know,' she said. 'He smelled terrible. Of fish and beer, and . . . other things. Poor old man,' she said; 'poor stinky old man.' How brutal, the casual pity of the young.

'Shall we go home?' she said. Home? I said. Well, if you're ready to come back. If you're quite sure you've been out long enough. If you've no more social calls to pay. She sighed. 'I'm sorry I worried you,' she said. 'I'm sorry I moved beyond your frame, Richard.'

My frame?

'The window,' she said. 'I'm sorry I didn't stay in the picture, today.' Was this exasperation? Her voice betrayed nothing, neither irritation nor contrition. I watched her as she wandered down the sand, and followed just behind in a wounded silence.

I like to look at you, I said, catching up to her. There's nothing I'd rather look at. Everything else is just backdrop.

'The sunset?' she said. 'Or look at the sea.' On it washed and wished, senseless.

That being the subject of your own devotion, I said. It sounded petulant, and yet I think I meant to be cruel – can that be? That I meant to be cruel to her?

'I like to watch the sea, yes. I do. And then I come home to you; to your human face.'

You like the contrast?

'I wouldn't say that,' she said. 'The sea is a grouch today, too. Look at it, all shrugs and sighs.'

I'm not a grouch, I said, doing my best not to soften.

'Then why is your face that way?'

I'm sorry, I said. Hang-dog.

'I'm not sure your penitent face is better.' I hung my head, then, shaggy and grey, chided, chastened, ashamed of my penitent face. And then felt her hands on my skull; felt her draw it down to kiss the crown, a benediction.

'*I'm* sorry,' she said. 'Really. I'm sorry you were worried and you didn't know where I was. I'm a bit sad to be leaving so soon, there's only a few days left. I lost track of time. I get lost in the sea . . .' Please don't, I said.

'And I do like you looking at me.'

Do you? I asked.

'Of course. Of course I do,' she said gently, soothing, smoothing my hair. 'Do you really adore me so, Richard?'

Of course. Of course I do.

'Well come on then. Chase me home,' she said, and took off at a sprint over the wet sand, light-footed and laughing. She puts on lightness like a dancer, changing like the sky over the islands. I tripped and stumbled after, trying not to lose my footing, trying not to lose her in the gloom, thin trousers flapping in the vicious wind.

She made watery under-poached over-salted eggs as a peace offering and I wolfed them down. She watched me eat. She said, 'I made you a promise, remember?' I smiled, lips gummy, grateful, so easily placated. And yet, now that I am alone, I can't remember quite what it was that she promised, or when, or if she promised anything at all.

How utterly deep, how impenetrable, how dense the night is here. The wind lashes around us now; it batters at the walls, it wails in the chimney, screeches in the eaves, hammers at the window; it whines and howls out there in the dark and I, in the dark within, listen. The night seems to seep in. From the window, nothing to be seen, neither sea nor sky, only the sound of the waves crashing, the frenzied wind, the cold glass rattling against the tumult. The fire is flaring and guttering. It's late, and she is in the kitchen, she is singing to herself, singing to the sea, her voice as if borne in from the water. I cannot make out the words; half a hum, half a deep, thrumming song, low and sorrowing, an old hymn; drowned almost in the wind, it comes in snatches, plaintive, distant. There must be fishermen, out in the squall furling and thickening around them, struggling to find their way home; it is a voice to be wrecked on the rocks for. A voice to be charmed to sleep by, a faery's song, to bring fierce sweet dreams I would not choose to wake from. I miss her terribly, here in my circle of firelight, with her so near to me and out of reach. Now that I am alone, I can only think of that stinky old man on the beach; of prurient Bob and his pretty, wistful son; of the sidelong stranger on the path; of Mr Begg even and his bag of sweets and the old boatman that brought us here; and of all the other men who have known her or met her or even seen her once and of those who will have her when I'm gone. Of her father and all the secrets she hasn't told me; I haven't her future or her past either.

She is in the kitchen singing, and I am listening, striving to preserve these precious pieces of her, which are lost the moment they are sung.

If I could capture just one scrap of her song.

Monday

The gale galloped through the night, all along the coastline, whipping up the sea and massing purple rainclouds on its way inland; it did not cease, all through the darkest hours. I lay awake listening to it whistle and holler, the riot of it over the barren isle, and her quiet breath beside me. They call this wind a skreever, so I'm told, a name for some fiend – and that indeed is how it sounds. Some ancient, rag-winged, shrieking thing, rending and tearing at the scrub-dry heather; the hardy sheep, the stocky furry ponies and the stocky furry cows, all clinging to the earth or huddling in barns and waiting for it to pass over.

It huffed and puffed around the walls of our little stone house, and clawed about inside, in every corner, searching, a stealthy intruder restlessly riffling pages and poking into every cranny and crack, whickering through every crevice, searching, searching, frantic, thorough, ruthless; dislodging the quiet spiders clutching stubbornly to the rafters and watching as their webs tattered; breathing on the last glow of the embers before skirling up the chimney in a billow of ash. Nothing left unstirred. And she, while it roared and gusted around us, slept on. Curious girl;

her first restful night since we came here, when all about, the sea and the sky, so restless.

I lay awake for hours, on my back, listening, eyes open or closed, I could not tell, an equal darkness within and without. Our bed a berth in a boat, below deck, the sea pressing up at the window and rolling and moiling below us; the fish swimming by the glass indifferent; tiny shrimp coiling and stretching in meaningless Morse code; all the sightless glowing life of the ocean floating past. A Leviathan's eye, filling the porthole, peering in.

And in my mind's eye, for comfort, I studied the ceiling, the fine crack I have come to know that runs through the plaster, the frosted lampshade and the dusty insects lying dead in its bowl, invisible against the opaque glass in daylight but fly-spotting the light when the switch is flipped. I thought how insecure we are, how lost we are in this darkness; and I thought no, not lost, because she is still breathing beside me.

And I thought of her in the kitchen, slicing bread, quite needlessly wearing the apron that she found hanging on the back of the kitchen door. She puts it on like a costume, for the simplest tasks. It has a pretty red heart stitched on the chest to protect or conceal the mess of valves and chambers beneath. It makes her feel capable, she says. Wifely. I may buy her one to wear at home. But that is an impossibly incongruous thought now. We seem to have floated free of bonds, of home, of time. In bed, I felt my own heart beating, and hers, her precious heart, against my hand.

And I thought of the bowls and plates and the glasses that we'd left in the sink, the dishes on the draining board, the crumbs on the counter still unswept, a gift for Mrs Odie and her all-embracing censure (and can we be blamed for the disorder which will surely be left in the wind's wake, I wondered? Or will the house have been swept clean by it, thoroughly scoured out?).

And I thought of the heavy-curtained sitting room with its clay and stone and stitched menagerie of seals and seabirds, and the cut-glass bowl in the centre of the table which already has collected the detritus of our days, the tokens of existence, hers and mine, mingled there – three pennies and a pound, an elastic band, tiny shells chosen for their wet lustre, now dry and ordinary; a piece of smoothed green glass, a pen, a paperclip, two silver coins and a pair of dice – how did we acquire them? All bedded in a small drift of sand, for our pockets are always silted with it by the end of the day, and each emptying dredges up a few more grains.

I thought of the spoil she kept for me from her ruined castle; a disc, like a coin, spined all over with tiny spikes, with a hole in the middle as if made to be strung. How simple a skeleton can be. A poor harmless urchin, now rotted away or stripped of flesh by some relentless chomping predator; but predator is perhaps too quick and wily a word for those great acid jellies undulating over the seabed, taking their time, preying not upon one, in a deadly chase, but upon hundreds, mouth wide to allow any poor creature crossing its path to be sucked in unheeding. Rolling over and slurping them clean like the gristle and meat of a chicken's foot pulled through the lips. Patient and voracious, the way of the sea hunter. I thought of them down there, untouched by the storm.

I listened to the sea and thought of the boats and ships, the buoys bobbing, the beam of the lighthouse signalling danger and hope; I thought of setting out on that sea for home, I thought of my office, my work, so many miles distant in another time; and I turned over and under and saw it all submerged, my desk sinking down, drawers lolling open, streaming seaweed as it fell, I found myself down among the seals, the whales, the squid and narwhals, mermaids laughing at my efforts to catch at my papers as they turned to pulp; until it settled on the bottom, redundant, a wrecked ship, coral-crusted, beaded with tiny bubbles. Anemones, their brilliance dimmed in the night-sea, mere ghosts of blossom. And my thoughts were turned back by the tide to this shore.

I thought of the tale she told me of Hildaland – of the hidden, sinking Orkney isle where the Finfolk spend their summers, shrouded in bright mist and music. An unseen island, rising from the water, enchanted, uncharted, where the sea-king reigns, she says, beyond the sea's brim, where those handsome jealous fishermen make their home. The merman in his sand-strewn caverns, cool and deep; her forsaken father, his bones of coral made. All of that, below the crazed surface, unheeding, deep, deep below the turmoil of the storm, while she slept on quietly.

I reached for her. She barely woke.

At last, I must have slept.

It is, today, so I am told, an attry day, rashan' and rainan' . . . When I woke it was late but still dark, the blind for once closed and only a crack of grey light seeping in, and the wind still roaring. She slept on, well into the morning, and I lay beside her quietly, curled against her, my face in her hair. She made no move, no sound, not a murmur, and eventually I extricated myself carefully and made my way to the kitchen to discover that the wind, with an effortless snap, has severed us from civilisation; sometime in the night, the lines were cut.

So I set out into the storm, climbing up our path to the road for the stretch of perhaps twenty feet where there is phone reception, and called Mrs Odie. A few steps at a time unbeleaguered, and then blasted by the wind rushing over the crest of the hill, lancing through my pyjamas. She took a long time to answer. She picked up the phone and said her number, rather primly, as my mother used to do – to preserve her anonymity, she always said. You never knew who might be calling. I wonder why Mrs Odie should wish to protect her identity. She could be hiding anything.

I said, It's Professor _____. 'Oh, aye, Mr _____,' she said. I cannot tell if she means anything by this insistence on denying me my honorific. I said our power was out. She said 'Oh, aye?' I said I'm sorry to trouble you, Mrs Odie. I wasn't sure who I should call. 'That'll be back on soon enough,' she said, with unfounded certainty. Right, I said. Do you know how soon exactly? 'It'll no be long,' she said. 'Aye, soon enough.' I wondered about her reckoning of 'soon' and 'enough'. Not aloud. Aloud, I said, Oh, fine, right, thank you Mrs Odie. 'Ah'll come by in an oor or so,' she said. There's no need, no need at all, Mrs Odie, I shouted – the wind was rising – 'No bother,' she said, and the gale cut us off.

Well, good morning, I said, coming in harried and wind-torn to find my wife more or less awake and curled up on the sofa. 'Morning,' she said, 'have you been out? There's no power.' I know, I said. Mrs Odie says it will be back soon enough. In the scheme of things. She nodded, satisfied, curled herself tighter. I think she rather likes the idea, playing the crofter's wife, lighting her lamps, tending the hearth.

You slept well, I said, bending to kiss her head from behind. I thought you were never going to wake up. She stretched, her legs stiffening, her arms tight against my neck and pushing up at the air above me, and smiled. 'I know, I can't believe it. I slept right through. Except when you pestered me.' I pestered you?

'You woke me up,' she said. 'I was having a nice dream. And you woke me up to have your way with me.' Oh, I'm sorry, I said, only a little sarcastic. You didn't seem all that awake, actually. And what was this lovely dream that you were dreaming so quietly?

'I was swimming.' She yawned again happily. 'The island floated away in the night,' she said. 'There was a lovely sort of pale lilac mist and we sailed into it, and there were men in boats with lanterns hanging, watching, and the sea had turned to silver, and I dived in and when I came to the surface my skin was all silver.'

She related all this in a kind of trance, still wrapped in the bright mist of her sleep. I wondered if she'd seen her father's face there; one of those tall hard unsmiling men, plying his oars. She shrugged.

The wet westerly brought Mrs Odie blowing through the door late morning, exclaiming, 'Whit a gushel!', seemingly enlivened by the storm. She came laden with provisions. 'Thoo'll no venture far the day, Ah'd suppose; thoo'll wait til hid's glettan',' she said, by way of explanation for her offering, or perhaps in admonition – certainly, she seemed to direct this over my shoulder at my wife, bundled on the sofa in her nightgown and an enormous cardigan. She brought more eggs, a loaf, bere bannocks, salty-sweet fresh butter, 'reestit mutton' – dear Mrs Odie, a one-woman tourist attraction. Smoked meat and flat dark barley bread, as if hundreds of years had slipped back in the night. I paid her, for these unrequested goods; it somehow didn't seem possible to refuse them. 'Oh, thank you, how kind,' said my wife sweetly. Any day now, I expect the old crone to arrive proffering a half-red apple. 'Thoo've plenty lamps and coal and matches, noo?' she said. 'Ah'd mind the fire; mind thee're no smoked oot. Jist give a call if thee want anything bringing. Aye, yin's ferly a skreever. An attry day,' she muttered to herself as she swept and dusted, 'might as weel while Ah'm here,' she said, a song of censure almost comforting in its list and lilt, tilted at the sea and sky and the unmade, storm-tossed bed alike. 'Hop there's a glett, or the ferry'll no be sailing,' she said. And then out she went with her basket, with a bang of the wind-blown door. I turned to see my wife beaming, bright as the vanished sun, delighted.

I boiled a pan of water and made toast under the grill, lighting the gas perilously with a match. Bearing the plate and a mug of tea, I found her pulling on long socks and boots in the sitting room, pushing her falling hair behind her ears. 'Look at the sea!' she said, 'look at the rain!' It was hard, in fact, to distinguish one from the other. I pressed the mug into her hands. I said, Have some breakfast. Have some tea. Have some toast. I said hopelessly, Please put more clothes on if you're going out. She looked down in surprise at her attire, and laughed, and made her way to the bedroom, shedding cardigan and gown as she went, and I gathered them as I followed and stood in the doorway watching her, her clothes still bed-warm and musty under one arm, and holding out a buttered, jammy triangle in the other hand. I watched the long line of her spine, the awkward hopping dance she did to pull her knickers over her boots, roll her socks over her knees; skirt, T-shirt, jumper, coat; I went to her, put a hand on the small of her bent back to still her for a moment, held out the toast as she stood up; she snapped it between her teeth and said, mouth full, 'You coming?'

Perhaps in a while, I said. It's . . . it's an attry day, you know, I said. Maybe you should stay in this morning. 'An att-rry day,' she repeated, pleased, chewing and somehow rolling the r through her mouthful. 'Okay,' she said, 'I'll keep you company. Maybe I can help. I can be your inspiration.' If she only knew. She sat down by me at the sitting room window, removing her coat but not parting with it, making a nest of it around her.

We sat before the window all morning, reading, and looking up from time to time to watch the waves, the rain on the sea, the angered sky, wrapped up from the relentless rage of it in what seemed to me a cosy, peaceable indoor silence. With no trees to stir in it, the wind is not always immediately visible here, although it can be heard, roaring in with the waves and wheuing in the eaves; but adjusting one's gaze, it becomes possible to see the whirl and eddy and rush of it in the rain, which flouts convention utterly and refuses to fall downwards. She sat opposite me, eyes flickering, following each gust. But after an hour or two I became aware of an increasing agitation in her, little shiftings and sighs, playing with the pebbles she's brought in and ranged along the sill, distractedly, fidgeting and fiddling, twisting her hair.

'Do you think,' she asked eventually, 'there will be a glett?' A what? I said. 'A break. A lull. An intermission.' Ah, I said. A respite. Who knows?

Her fingers were actually drumming the sill, a slow tattoo. Each long thin bone in turn stretching the skin on the back of her hand, tight across the bridge of her knuckles; tension taut and twanging like over-wound catgut. Lifting a shell to her ear. 'I can hear the sea,' she said. Could it be, I said, that perhaps it is really the sea you are hearing, not the echo of a shell?

'Maybe. I hope it stays stuck there, when we . . .' and she trailed off, looking into the smooth pink hollow of it. We'll take it home with us, I said. We'll carry the sound of the sea with us.

She twisted and fiddled, a snap of nervous energy, restless as the wind fretting at the window. Strange light filtered through the massing clouds, the sky and the sea churning.

After a pause of perhaps ten further fidgety, fiddly minutes, she put down her mug and said, 'Shall we go out, then, just for a little while?' I set down my pen, with a short sigh, perhaps; looked at her, I suppose, as if she was mad. She looked back as if she wasn't, as if she didn't think so; but betrayed by that agitated dancing behind her clouded eyes. Feeling cooped up? I asked. I recited: Or narrow if needs the house must be, outside are the storms and strangers; we . . . She smiled with half of her mouth. Thee and me? I prompted. I gave up. You go on, I said. I'll keep an eye on you. You go. And she went.

A room without her in it. Just the faintest static flicker of impatience left behind her. So she stands there again, alone, impossible, watching as the waves leap and thrash; she can barely stand at all, yet holds her ground, making little side-staggers to right herself against the wind, which presses her coat so close against her that it could be another skin. The long thigh, the bone-jut of her hip, her narrow waist that I can almost circle, not fragile but strong and serpentine, twisting in my grip.

I wish she would come in. But she'll stay there I think until the tide comes for her, or I do.

There she stands, a violet-grey smear against the saturated horizon. Washed through so that I can almost see the squalling sea right through her. The rain on the glass streaking her image. Woman resolving into water. Undine, returning to her element. Any bright rivulet might be her. Any or none. No longer my wife but just a ghost made of rain, an elemental returning to form. And I find myself asking, who is that woman who stands heedless on the beach? Can she be my wife?

Spreading her hands out in front of her and turning her face up and the water pouring around and through her, and I wonder if she might dissolve, disperse into the water and be washed out with the tide, and I wonder, if she were, if I or anyone would believe she ever existed at all.

The wild waves, rearing and pounding.

The wind-whipped sky.

My wife. The storm-witch on the shore.

*

I watched her watching for an endless hour, less, perhaps; and quite suddenly the sky went from purple to black, lowered as if

to crush her, the black tide rushing; she climbed up to the rocks,
I watched as she spread her arms wide. She staggered, leaning
into the wind; lost and found her footing; I saw her fall. I cried
her name, useless behind the streaked glass, I stood and called
her name and couldn't see her, could barely make her out at all. I
should not have let her go alone. I pulled my shoes on desperately
and dashed out as I was, in just a sweater, out into the storm; as
I rounded the corner of the house I felt the blast of the sea-wind,
smashing into my chest. And I thought, How could she possibly
have stayed standing so long, how is it that she is so strong? I
pushed on, over the links, every inhalation snatched by the gale,
forcing my way through the tar-thick dark, my torch sweeping
the rocks like a feeble lighthouse beam, and I saw her laid out on
her back there, laid out on the rocks, and laughing, crazed, hair
splayed out around her like the corona of a fallen moon. I could
hear only the faintest echo of her in the gale; I went to her, knelt
beside her, cried out to her, but even her own name could not
reach her. I clasped her shoulders and then her eyes flew open,
and stared up at me wide and unfrightened, when I could hardly
keep mine open at all; the sea now was rushing onto the rocks,
reaching for her feet, far beyond the tide-line in its grasping fury,
and she didn't seem to care until I shouted, The sea! Stand up!
Look at the sea! And she sat up then and gasped as if waking
and I helped her stand and she gripped on to me hard enough to

hurt me, and I felt the night had come to overwhelm us, and we might drown in one of her dreams. I raised her up and led her, staggering against the wet, the wind, the slippery weed, until at last we reached the grass, and we put our heads down and forced our way on, drenched with the vicious scour of salt and sand; I thought I heard her call out, I turned and could barely make out her face, her cheeks sea-streaked or tear-stained, streaming black with mascara I didn't know she wore, as if she were crying coal-dust. I yelled, We're nearly there; she let out a thin, exhilarated scream.

We reached the side of the cottage and were thrown around the corner of it, the wind tunnelling, and reached the door at last. She skittered inside like a dry leaf, the only leaf on this treeless isle, blown in on a foreign breeze, and I forced the door shut against the storm and secured the catch and the room whirled around us and resettled, papers shifting and lifting, a panting all through the house as it caught its breath and exhaled; her hair whipped into twisted hawsers that my fingers would later tug in. I took her in my arms and she stood with fists bunched against my chest and I gripped her wrists; she was breathless, all the energy of the tempest unleashed and crackling around her; I looked down at her, and she looked wild, thrilled and terrified, her face still wet from the sea-spray, her storm-light eyes wide with the mad wind. Her hands so cold, and she didn't seem to notice. Was this the same girl who doodled in her margins and blushed at my office door? I remembered the day she came in from the rain, so calmly . . . You scared me, I said. You could have hurt yourself. Did you hurt yourself? You could have been blown away. Please don't do that again. I was pleading, my voice shaking with a waver of panic that I couldn't control. Promise you won't leave like that again. 'You could have come with me,' she said. I'm sorry, I said. I know. But I came for you. Please don't do it again.

She didn't answer, but detached herself, and slid out from between my body and the door, and said, 'I'm soaked,' and took off her coat and let it fall, and took off her sweater and dropped it, and unhooked her skirt and stepped out of the damp ring of it, and stood there in bra, knickers and high-laced boots with a darkening, gathering cloud of a bruise at the top of her thigh where she'd fallen. I went to her and touched it, gently, and she pulled my hips in to her and wound her cobweb hair about my neck, murmured, 'You promise you'll stay. With me.' Of course. Of course I will. For as long as I can I'll be with you. Come to the fire, I said. Come back to me, come up from the deep. And she kissed me fiercely then, the storm still in her; the gale raging without, the waves clutching at the shore empty-handed; close, safe, warm inside.

I and she.

I tended to the fire while she lit candles. I fiddled with the oil-lamps, their greasy wicks smearing the glass. 'Does it remind you of when you were little? Before electricity?' she asked, and I wasn't sure if she was joking. I made for the kitchen, and felt her approach, silent, behind me; her arms circled my waist, and I led the way; like children not wishing to be alone, we travelled together in this truncated conga line. We ate by lamplight at the solid table, bread, cheese, soup from a tin. It was salty.

We took the bowls to the sink, together; and there we were, in the window, the candle throwing our images upon the black pane; two gaunt creatures, all pale and wan, dark-socketed, hollow-cheeked; ageless in the amber light. Cadaverous, but well-matched. We heated hot milk with honey (her whim) and whisky (mine). We sat in front of the fire, the wild night all around us. We are quite out of time. It could be the present, or any time in the last thousand years of the past. The wind whistled in the flue; the fire flickering and leaping, by turns enthused and unsure, but remaining alight. I loaded on coals. When the fire in a croft went out, she says, it meant the life was gone from that house. She says that it's bad luck to whistle, to imitate the wind; she says that if a glass sounds a note when no one has touched it, it means a death at sea. I dipped my finger, ran it around my tumbler. She gripped my hand, harder than I have ever felt those strong cold fingers grip. 'Don't,' she said. Then licked the whisky from my fingertip and laughed.

The wind battered at the door. She says that on nights like this, suitors come knocking. The selkie men looking for a dalliance; she says they're always after the new brides. She says the seal-folk are beautiful, beguiling, and must be guarded against with charms, with a lock of her hair above the door; she says I'd best take care or they'll come knocking, and lift the latch and let themselves in as if they've a right to shelter, however fast the door is barred. 'Don't let them take me into the water,' she said, half laughing. What if he's really attractive? I asked, trying to play along. A real catch-of-the-day. She snorted. She says if a woman wants a selkie man, she must cry seven tears into the tide and he'll come. I said, I won't allow it. He's not taking you anywhere.

She says that while the selkies are gentle, the finfolk too are notorious seducers, but less kind; the tall, gaunt sea-farers with narrow faces and hard dark eyes, who rule the seas in these parts and will guide you safe, for a fee of silver. She says they come ashore sometimes, to seek new wives upon the land. And when they've had their fill, away they sail, back into the mists. But, she says, they always come back, to reclaim the little webbed daughters they've fathered on the land, to take them back to the sea-king's realm; in the end, they'll come back for their own. And she raised and splayed her hand. I laughed, uneasily, unsure if in some way she believes this. She says they don't draw the same distinctions, here, between histories, stories and myths; she said this as if to an outsider, looking in.

And what are the women up to, while their men are out on the land, strewing their salty seed, I asked? 'Ah, well,' she said. 'Do you want to hear a story? It's my turn, I think.' I do, I said eagerly. 'Do you want to know what's drawn the men from their homes, what it is they've let the fire go cold for?'

Like our neighbour's, I said. There was no fire in that house. All these abandoned houses.

'Right. Like that.' She nodded. 'Okay, so: here's a story for your book.' And she leaned against the sofa and reached for her glass. 'This is a tale of Finfolkaheem,' she said, her voice modulating to a soft, low lilt, traced with the trill and roll of the sea, that echo of her father's accent; 'this is a tale of the city beyond the sea's brim, the home of the sea-king, and of the beautiful, cruel finfolk, who guard these waters jealously, and love silver.' I arranged myself comfortably, filled our glasses – we were in need of the warmth – and she began, staring into the flames, as if reading the tale there.

There was, it seems, a crofter, a broad, bold, strong young man, honest of heart and innocent. Much like myself, in many ways, I suggested. 'Innocent?' she said, smirking, but would allow, it seemed, 'young'; 'Shush,' she said. 'One afternoon, when the harvest was lately gathered and the sun shining, this crofter – let's call him, I don't know, Donald? Will that do?' And she fell back into the story, into the lull of her own voice. 'This autumn afternoon, Donald went down to the rocky shore to look for limpets for his dinner. And when he'd nearly filled his bucket, he saw, holding fast to an outcrop jutting over the water, a cluster of mountainous shells bigger than any he'd yet collected, bigger than any he'd ever seen, and being of a healthy appetite, this brawny, brave lad, imagining the fat, fleshy bite between his teeth, he left his bucket at the base of the outcrop and scrambled up to lie full stretch upon it, to prise his prize from the rock, his face and his arms hanging over the edge.

'And so intent was he upon the stubborn limpets, that he didn't see the water below swirl and turn silvery until he became aware of a note, a note so profound it seemed to come from the depths of the sea and go right down to the depth of himself; it filled his heart, it sang like blood in his ears, so that he thought he'd faint – and just as his vision closed in, swirling down, down into that whirl of water, he saw two white arms reach out to him, and felt them grasp his shoulders, and was pulled under, into the water, and blackness.' She took a gulp of whisky; I waited for her to go on; the crackling silence warm within, the storm outside.

'When he woke, he found himself sprawled in the bottom of

a wooden boat; opposite him, the sun setting behind her, a woman of prodigious beauty, naked, her shining hair hanging over her breasts, her white skin, and her belly glistening with the first of the silvery scales that covered her hips, and further down still' – Good Lord, I said, Donald's not shy – 'poor innocent Donald, he couldn't help but look,' she said, 'he'd never seen a woman without her clothes before . . . but this was no woman, for the curve of her hips formed the base of a strong silver tail, hanging over the side of the boat and propelling them on into the sunset. And turning to look behind, Donald could see no sign of the islands, no land rising from the darkening sea, and despite the mermaid's beauty, despite her tender smile, he was afraid then, and wished only to return to his simple home and hearth, and he thought of his bucket of limpets left on the beach, and opened his mouth to ask her to turn, but found he had no words. And then she leaned towards him and kissed his open lips, and poured her breath like honey into him, and he was no longer afraid, because with that, he was in love.'

Like when you kissed me, I said. 'You kissed *me*,' she said. 'But anyway, sh. Listen: she kissed him, and he wasn't afraid any longer. And when she bent to unlace his boots, his good, sturdy boots that had seen him through the work of five summers, through five harvests and five long winters too, when she unlaced them and pulled them from his unresisting feet, when she tossed them in the water, he made no objection. "You must enter my home barefoot," she told him, "if you care to come there with me."' She might have asked before taking his shoes, I said. 'She knew he would come,' she said. 'She knew, by then, that he loved her.' She looked into her glass, now empty, and held it out. I filled it obediently.

'She looked to the stars; only then did Donald notice it had grown dark; and her eyes sought out the brightest, and glittered with its light, and she guided them beneath it, and all at once a whirlpool opened up in the calm sea's surface and down they went, boat, crofter and mermaid all, in a great twist of water, and when they landed on the seabed Donald found, to his amazement, that he had no need to breathe. And before him was a vast, shimmering city of bones and pearl and silver, with sharks' teeth topping the walls and a whale's jaw for a gate. And the mermaid, who walked now on two feet, two legs fine and strong and supple, took him by the hand and led him through the gate into Finfolkaheem. And she led him through the silver city, and at its centre was a grand hall, a hall of crystal, hung with drapes that flashed and crackled like the merry dancers in the northern sky, pink and pale green and golden; and he was seated at the head of a long table with his new love, who was the Princess of that realm, and a great feast was served. And at the end, the sea-king raised the spiral shell he drank from, and blessed their union, and with that, Donald was forever betrothed to the sea-king's daughter. And then the finfolk danced, and he loved them for their elegance, their stately, solemn movements, these tall, pale, taciturn creatures. And of them all, he loved his new wife best, the most gracious and lovely of all.' I know how he feels, I said; saccharine Richard. Nevertheless, she kissed me, and went on:

'When the dancing was over, she led him to her bedchamber, and he swept each lock of her hair from her so that she lay with it spread all around her, and if he had been breathing then, he would have held his breath, as he slowly, slowly revealed her . . .' She described the tickle and trail of her hair and her cool skin against him, this poor innocent virgin boy, how he felt her all around him, she said, and was lost in her for hours of breathless silence until at last he gave in to her with a soundless shudder . . . By now I confess I was pawing at her, at the trailing strands of her long hair, my breath, too, caught in my throat. And still, she went on:

'And time passed, unnumbered days, for there is no day or night in Finfolkaheem; the water is permeated always with the glow of phosphorescence, and lit in streaks and flashes by tiny electric fish. Donald existed in a wash of bliss, of wine and feasting, and hunting with the powerful finmen and their packs of seals, riding their seahorses on the crest of a wave, searching out their prey through the vast forests of wrack, and returning always to her arms; he was lost to pleasure and love, enchanted by the strange, soft, melancholy music which sang always through the city, and he had quite forgotten his croft, his farm, the gathered harvest and the new crops left unsown, the sheep growing shaggy, the hearth long since cold, and his bucket of limpets left on the shore.'

And she smiled, and drained her glass, and held it at eye level thoughtfully. Is that the end? I asked. He doesn't ever go back? 'Well,' she said, 'I was looking through that book you got from Mr Begg, and in that version there was some business with a black cat, sent by a witch, a spae-wife, to free him – I suppose they found his bucket on the beach and wondered what had become of him. The cat seizes his finger with its paws and makes him draw a cross on the mermaid's brow and that breaks the charm. It's all a bit silly.' And what then? I asked. 'He returns to his island, and marries the spae-wife's niece, and is eternally grateful to her for releasing him and inevitably, so the story says anyway, lives happily ever after.'

Grateful? I said. But he truly loved the mermaid? 'Yes.' And was happy there, in Finfolkaheem? 'Very happy.' Then what right did the old witch have to spoil his happiness? And why did he allow it? 'Some men don't take kindly to bewitching, I suppose,' she said. Some men, I said, are idiots, and don't deserve to be bewitched. 'Well, quite,' she said. I prefer your version, I told her. 'Me, too,' she smiled. 'That's how I was told it.'

I asked, How do you come to know these stories? She shrugged. 'I just seem to know them.'

Her father, telling her stories by the side of her box bed. It is perhaps absurd, how I resent him, for getting there first.

The night of her birth must surely have been one such as this; she can only be a child of a storm, of a wild tide. The tempest raging at the window, clamouring for her; her mother pale and grim. The tide smashing the shore, a full moon paling the clouds; the wind howling, stamping, clattering, baying for entry to snatch her away; she was surely meant for a changeling, some sickly wizened thing left in the place of this perfect, silver-bright and canny girl. But her father saw her safe into the world, and she bawled fit to beat the wind, I bet, or else merely wriggled and laughed.

And I, where was I? Impossible to know, now, what I was doing, unwitting, as my intended came into being. Far from the storm, no doubt safely inland, marking papers perhaps or reading, pencil in hand, resting a mug on the ring-stained arm of my one comfy chair. Is it possible that not even the faintest echo of her first cry reached me, that I didn't feel some change, some quickening in the world run through my nerves?

Her father wipes the blood from her; from this moment on he has no eyes for her mother, lying hollowed out and papery as the skin of a snake. He sings her a song, a song from the sea in an old language; he spreads her little clutching hands and smiles. Feels her tiny webbed fingers grip his long ones. Strokes the silvery down on her head. And as her mother wastes and pales into sadness, cruelty and gall, he dandles her on his knee, feeds her when her mother won't take her to her breast, stands at the window with her and points out to the sea – the winter storms, the fickle spring tides, the silvered summers. He tells her about the sea-mither, the goddess of the isles; quick to anger, unpredictable, fierce and kind and bounteous. He tells her of the finfolk and the selkies. Nothing can replace those first tales, which have coloured the cast of her thought, which have filled her nights with the sea, and which are at least as real to her as anything she's learned of the world since. For all her brilliance – or perhaps this is the source of it – she is still that child listening quietly. Is that what she asked to come here for, to recover some lost tale, the sound of her father's voice in the sea? Nothing I can tell her will ever sound in her so deep.

He teaches her words, and strings them into stories like sea-pearls. Then one day, vanishes.

She says the finmen always come back for their own.

Tuesday

Have you always been a sleepwalker? I asked over breakfast, as she squashed a bacon sandwich flat between her fingers. 'What?' she said. 'I'm not.' But . . . She gave me a funny look, quizzical, doting, dear senile Richard, and licked brown sauce off her knuckle.

'You mean last night? I was awake,' she said. 'I saw a ship, a white ship. I was watching it.' But . . . I stopped. You were awake? I said. 'Of course. I talked to you.' Yes, but . . . you said you saw a ship. You were dreaming of a ship. 'No,' she said. 'I *saw* a ship. You were muttering in your sleep, it woke me up. I got up to get water and I looked out and saw a ship. You know, I can't even remember what I dreamed.' She frowned for a moment, shrugged.

But there was no ship, and if there had been, she couldn't possibly have seen it in the darkness; the lighthouse illuminating nothing but the rain as it thinned.

I woke in the night from a half-dream of salt water filling nose and mouth and lungs; something twining round me, water filling every artery, pulsing blue brine; breathing water and stretching for the surface and waking with a gasp so familiar that I took it at first to be hers. But when I reached for her she wasn't there and it was I that had been wrenched from the deep, this time, and she wasn't there to comfort me; an empty sensation, like waking with hunger or cold. I called for her; she didn't answer.

I crept from the bedroom, I listened at the bathroom door; no crack of candlelight and no sound of water. I said her name; no answer. She was not in the kitchen either; outside, the beach was dark; nothing to be seen from the window, only darkness where the sea must be, only the sound of it, the rain and the gale battering. Everything silent within but for the wind, creaking and creeping in, blowing cold draughts on my neck, my ankles. I found her at last at the sitting room window, reflected in the pane, and quite still. A monochrome world; the cosy homestead made unhomely, enchanted, a colour plate overlaid with tissue, made grey. She had a hand to the glass, just the tips of her fingers, I could see white at the knuckles where the blood was pressed out with the pressure. A silent gesture I couldn't comprehend. The night was blustering at the window. I stood behind her, covered her hand with mine, pressed myself against her back; not wanting to wake her, but fearing that she'd catch a chill. I bowed my head and breathed warmth on her neck, my nose under the ridge of her skull. She was all bone, white and cold. She didn't move, she didn't turn, she didn't speak. I strained to listen for her breath. I couldn't feel it under me.

I said her name. I said her name into her neck. I prised her hands from the window and I turned her to me and her eyes were glass, dark-sheened; although she seemed to look at me, she didn't see me, and it wasn't to me that she spoke.

She said, 'There was a white ship. Sailing on the path that the moon made on the water. I came to watch.' But the hidden moon's light was scattered by the scattering cloud, the sea was glinting with knives of it in the blackness, and there was no ship and nothing to see it by. I led her back to bed. She was unresisting, listless. She shivered and sighed and snuggled into the cave I made for her, the bones of her shins resting on my thighs, her knees pressing into my stomach. How long were you standing there? I asked.

'I don't know,' she said. 'I'm cold,' she said, with a spasm, drawing breath through her teeth. I know, I said. Your hands are like ice. She pulled them away and whispered 'sorry' and I gripped them, pulled them back, pressed them flat to my chest under mine until I thought my blood would freeze over as it pulsed out of my freezing heart. You were dreaming, I said. In the night, she didn't deny it.

'There was a ship,' she said, 'out at sea. Coming for me. I had to leave.' Did you want to go? I asked. 'I was meant to. I felt I had to. But I didn't want to leave you,' she said. 'I wanted to stay . . .'

I want you to stay, I said. Why don't we just stay. 'Here?' she said. Together, I meant. Anywhere, I said. With me. I heard her heave a breath and let it out again all ragged, fractured, as if she had been weeping, although I had heard no tears.

I don't think I slept, the rest of the night. I listened to her breathe. A mutter, a sigh. I listened to the wind calming, the roar of it quieting to a low growl, stalking about the house as an animal crouching, hind-quarters tense and ready, waiting to pounce. By the time we rose, it was almost noon and the storm was in abeyance; the gloom beyond the window kept us to our bed, dozing, and sometimes not. She was snoozy and sweet all morning, at her most pliable. Eventually she suggested, as I nibbled at her knuckles, that if I was hungry, I should make us breakfast. 'I'm ravenous,' she said. 'Starving. Practically malnourished. I could eat a pig.' Bacon sandwich? 'That'll do, I suppose,' she said.

Out on the beach now she keeps watch, but there is no sign of a sail. She is a huddle on the shore, like some fluff-feathered bird hunkered into the puff of itself, only her white face protruding from the mass of garments. I can see almost nothing of her, balled up there – not a jut of a joint or a wisp of silver.

It is a dismal, chilly day, and instead of feeling cosy and cosseted indoors, I feel myself half in the mist that is encroaching, thickening over the water; it hasn't lifted. The low sun is a perfect pale disc without halo or shine, a hole-punched circle in a parchment sky. The storm has left a faded world behind, the cliffs, the sea, the neighbouring island, each a flat cut-out layered up in transparent shades of grey. Everything slightly damp to the touch. All is without contour, bland, dreary, a world heavy as lead. Nothing stirring, not even hardly the water. It neither advances nor retreats; it has made just the barest, hesitant approach up the shore towards her, an inch or two at most, and she regards it flatly, and it has barely the energy to nudge at the sand. As if all the energy has been sucked up and swallowed by the deadened sea, in which I imagine the fishes, the whales, even the mermaids, floating bored, wall-eyed, flipping a listless fin once in a while for the sake of appearances, without propulsion.

The lamplight seems soaked up. Everything that casts a light is ghosted. And she is little more than a tracery of faded ink. She seems, each day that passes, to blend into the light and the changing skyline, so that it would seem cruel, somehow, to remove her.

I sit with my books before me but pay them scant attention. I can afford to let the time slide. I am waiting for the moment to tell her: I will devote myself to her only from hereon. I won't be going back to my job. I shan't teach any more – what pupil could possibly follow her? I'll take down the plaque from my door; let some other poor fool's mail get stuffed into the pigeonhole that for thirty years has borne my name. No more tedious tutorials, no more endless execrable essays. Enough. Let it all go. How cosy it could be, the ermine mantle of the Professor Emeritus. I will work away at my book, with her help perhaps, but the School will do without me, and we will go wherever she wishes to be.

So I will end my career with a fade out, a sabbatical that will now stretch beyond this term to an indefinite end – a fullness of time, filled with her. I thought I'd be stowed away in that dingy office of mine for years yet; they'd find me there, all dust and bones, deep in the basement and quite forgotten, clutching a biro, dead mid-sentence. Such is the fate from which she has saved me, which strange to say I had almost looked forward to, before I met her.

Still she has mentioned no plans beyond the end of this honeymoon, and I suppose I have forgotten to ask, or given up asking. Perhaps she means never to leave here; perhaps she means to go on staring out for the rest of her days. And if that is so then I shall remain, Calypso's willing captive on Ogygia, waiting upon my deity; and if I only stay at her side, she will keep me immortal. I am Circe's happy pig on Aiaia; I have made it to the Sirens' shore and am happily stranded, drugged with love as with the lotos, a slumbering, lumbering love, lolloping round the island, circling her, happily circumscribed. With no need for future or past. I am growing accustomed to the shadowy corners, the indistinct shapes; there is no sign of our power being restored. We will go to bed early, or drink by the fire, close together, for warmth; it could be worse. I can live with this darkness. I could live in this half-light beside her, out of time, indefinitely, despite the cold. If she would only come in.

The seals are out today, looking unhappy in the mizzling rain. Sad sacks of taut skin, occasionally craning their heads and flopping back down again, disconsolate. Although they seem to look unhappy in any weather; tearful, fearful creatures. We have often seen them out, barking, each to each; but they rally and stir the moment we draw near, first one and then the whole herd of them belly-flopping frantically down to the sea as fast as their little stunted flippers can carry them. But today, while she has been sitting, I have seen one, two, a dozen little wet-whiskered, doggy heads poking out of the foam. And as I've watched, one after another they've broached the shore, looking shifty despite their ungainly gait, and they have formed ranks on either side of her, at a safe distance, and appear to be watching, ever cautious. And as she has barely moved, one of the fearless pups has made a waddling advance towards her, and the adults must follow to defend it; several, now, are quite close. That little chocolate brown one could eat from her hand, if she happened to have a morsel of fish to offer. She does not reach out, however, and it does not come closer; just watches with those pooly dark eyes, wet, empty and shining, and I can see, I think, her lips moving, and the little selkie sits and listens.

I am not quite warm enough, cold in my clothes, displaced, a shiver on my chest.

I stare at the page. The letters swim and fail to reassemble. Rub and pinch the bridge of my nose, press the nostrils together.

The sky lowering; closing in like rising water. Sinus pressure below the eyes. Clouds coming down heavy like sleep.

I thought I heard her say my name.

But she's still out there, I think; I think I can make her out. For a moment I lost her against the sky; and then she turned her head and came back into being, silver flaring in the dull light.

Pale arms reaching, out of the water.

*

It is already growing dark, at three o'clock. I am not sure where the day has gone; the sun seems barely to have risen, and now darkness is falling. It has crept into the corners of the room behind me, and she is increasingly hard to discern against the dimness. I must light candles to see by, to guide her home, presenting a haven to her in the dark.

In the kitchen I peel potatoes carefully, carefully ignite the hob with a candle, boil them and reheat a leftover mutton stew and give thanks for it; the storm-rations of Mrs Odie's basket will tide us over another night. At least there is wine left. And whisky for dessert.

I stand at the window and raise my candle and hope to beckon her home.

*

Were her cheeks streaked only from the sea, when she came in? Her skin was chill and damp to the touch and paler than ever. Were you crying? I asked. I wiped at her cheek, put my thumb to my lips. 'Seven tears to call a selkie man,' she said, with seeming lightness. I harrumphed. No sign yet, I take it? When might we expect your new suitor? She laughed. 'Just the cold, and the wind. No tears were shed. Not one.'

Well then, what did that little brown seal have to say? I asked. 'Not much,' she said. 'They're secretive creatures.' They run off whenever I get near them, I said. 'They probably smell you,' she said. What do I smell of? Is it all that offensive? I asked, mock-indignant; but supposing I become one of those old men, nostrils too clogged with curling grey hair to smell their own odour, of coffee breath, of unwashed wool, of bowels? 'Of man,' she said. A relief. 'Of murder.' What could she mean?

I've no blood on my hands, I said. 'Of course not. But they don't know that. All they know, from experience, is that to the likes of you they are just meat and blubber and oil, all bagged up in a convenient, valuable, waterproof packaging. Which they prefer to keep wearing.' What about you, then, I said; how is it that you come up smelling of roses? Or fish or whatever it is they'd rather I smelled of? 'I don't smell of fish,' she said. No, I said, no, of course you don't. You smell of the sea. Of deep water. And of biscuits. 'I what? How do I smell of biscuits?' I don't know, I said humbly. You just do. Of salt and oats. She looked bemused. 'I'm a woman,' she said. 'Maybe that's it. Maybe I smell of kindness, not killing.'

Ah yes, I said. One of those kind, meek and gentle Northern females, who never threaded sinew through a bone needle; that must be what they're smelling. She conceded the point. 'I don't know. I've been out there for days, I suppose they're used to me. They know me. Maybe they think I belong here.' Ah, could it be that they will tempt you at last to take to the sea with your suitor, my little selkie? She frowned. 'Not likely. Can't swim yet.'

I laid the table and we ate by candle-light. The night held at bay beyond the window, our doubles projected upon it; the cosy interior scene made strange by the outside dark that lurked behind it. She swiped the last of the gravy from her plate and then mine with a finger and sucked it clean with a smack of her lips and smiled. She took up the candle and led me with it to the fireside, and kneeled and pulled me down to her and put her arms around me under my shirt and her legs around my waist and although her hands were as cold as ever, in the circle of her I felt warm again.

'What have you been working on today, then, Professor? Do you have a story for me?' she asked, once settled, wrapped in a rug with a glass in hand. What have I been working on? The day has been swallowed up by the grey. I've no idea what I've been doing. Watching her. Watching out for ships in the mist. I may have been sleeping. A memory of something reaching; or was this just a vision from a dream?

Just checking references today, I said. Nothing to report. No mention of the future seemed fitting, in the firelight. 'In that case, I've got another one,' she said. 'Listen – here's the selkie's story.' Ah! I knew it, I said. I knew you'd had some secret from him. That sly little pup.

'So,' she said. 'There was a young crofter.' Oh yes, I know the type, I said. Another of your brawny limpet-pickers, is it? 'This one's different. Do you want to hear, or not?' she said. By all means, I said. Please, go on. 'Thank you,' she said.

This particular crofter, she explained, was lonely; he worked his land hard, alone, and took out his boat to fish, and kept his small flock and a horse and a cow, but there was no one but him to milk her, and no one to tend the fire in his hearth, and he slept each night with only his dog to warm him.

And one day, as he was gathering kelp on the shore, he heard music from the sea and saw three women, naked on the rocks, combing their brown, their red, their blonde hair. 'And each was beautiful, and they combed one another's hair and sang, each to each,' she said; 'and the crofter fell at once in love with the golden one.' Surely it was silver, I said, not golden. Surely he fell for the flash of her silver hair. 'Very well,' she smiled; 'he loved the grey one.' Argent, pearly, opaline, I insisted. 'Ash, hoar, stone,' she said. 'Grey. May I go on?' Yes, yes, go on, I said. The lonely crofter fell in love with the silver-headed girl.

'So the crofter watched quietly from the shore; but his dog didn't seem to take too well to their song, and barked and yapped and ran back and forth at the edge of the water, and the women were startled and slipped from their rock, and the crofter ran down the beach, pulling his shirt off, ready to dive and save them although it was bitter cold and he couldn't swim. But just as he reached the water, he saw three sleek heads emerging, and three seals, a bronze, a dark and a pale one, turned in the waves and swam out.

'The crofter's heart was as heavy as his load of kelp as he turned for home. On his path he met Old Thomas; lame Old Thomas, not a tooth in his head, reeking of whisky, but wise.' She filled our glasses. She raised a silent toast, to Thomas. 'And Thomas told the crofter that the ladies he had seen were the daughters of the King of Lochlann, from beyond the sea's brim, and explained what the crofter must do if he wished to capture a sea-princess, when the selkie women came back.' This part of the story, it seems, is uncertain; in nine days' time, or at the next full moon, or a year to the day, the crofter must return to the beach.

'So the lovelorn crofter waited,' she went on, 'and when the time came he returned to the beach. And again, as he came down to the shore he heard music, and the women, again, were singing, but this time Angus' – Angus? I said. 'The dog. I think it's a good name for a dog . . . Angus was left tied by the barn door to howl at the moon unheard and alone. And the crofter crept quietly down to the beach and crouched, hidden, waiting, and watched in wonder as they slipped from their perch. And this time, with no Angus to scare them off, the three seals swam into shore, lithe and easy in the water. And as they reached the beach, they slipped out of their silken seal's skin on the sand, and emerged three women again, pale and lovely, and the crofter watched carefully where they stowed their bundles, behind the rocks. And the women danced to the music of their father's kingdom, a slow, mysterious dance, on the shore in the full moonlight, to which they answer, like the tide that brought them ashore.' So it is the full moon, then, that brings them? I asked, glancing out of the window at the moon rising, close to full but not quite, the room lit silver and shadowed away from the light of the fire. 'Yes,' she said. 'I like that version. And he needs a light to see by. So, he crept around the rocks, and saw, in the moonlight . . .' and now she turned too, to look out at the near-roundness of it, fat and haloed and diffuse in the velvet, rain-washed sky; '. . . by the full moon's light he could see that one of the furs was glowing brightly, almost white. And he gathered it up and stood, and the selkie women stopped dancing, and the grey-haired one cried, Oh please, give me back my skin, but the crofter would not, and walked away from them, knowing she must follow, because if her skin is stolen,' she whispered, 'she can never return to the sea. And she followed, at a distance, and he did not once turn, so that he didn't have to see her weep. But he could hear her, and as they left the roar of the sea behind them, she wept louder and bitterly, until it was the only sound he could hear. And still, he did not turn, until they reached his little house and she followed him in.'

The crofter hides the skin, and the next day she asks for it, and he refuses; and after that she doesn't ask again, and no longer weeps, and marries him. He gives her a name, because she won't reveal her own. She eats only raw fish, at first, with her hands. Having guests is awkward. But she learns to eat it boiled or smoked, with a fork, and becomes a good wife, and bakes his bread and milks the cow and cooks his porridge in the morning and his soup when he comes home from his labour, although she does not eat with him; she keeps the hearth burning, and a pot upon it, and is warm and smooth-skinned in the bed at night. And poor old Angus never quite trusts her, but consents to sleep at their feet.

'She neither wept, nor laughed, nor sang, but she was loving, for twenty years, and bore him seven children, who all loved to swim in the sea; until one day, their youngest son came upon a salty, stinky, dried-out bundle, hidden in the wall of the barn; and when he brought it to her, at last she laughed and wept, and the boy watched as she took it to the shore; he watched as his mother shed her clothes and dived into the water with her bundle and vanished; and then he saw, for a second, a white head emerge from the waves and a sad seal's gaze looking back at him. And to this day, every full moon after, he comes to the beach with his father, to hear the selkies sing. And the crofter and his family, when they take their boat out, haul fish in abundance; and he can only be glad of the years he had, because as that old sot Thomas warned him, a wild creature will always go back to the wild.'

That's rather sad, I said. 'He got twenty years out of her,' she said, reasonably, and then looked away, and busied herself with poking at the fire. Can she hope for as much? And how could that possibly be enough? All the more reason to give her every minute.

I couldn't think of a way to fill the silence. 'And lots of fish,' she said. She filled her glass and laughed.

Now she sings in the mist that she's conjured about her in the bathroom, drifting salt-scented through the house with her song; I sit in the half-dark and listen to her singing to herself, singing to the sailors, and I can't stop thinking of those strange half-selkie children in her story, yearning for the water, unable to live there. Suppose we were to bring our own little pups into the world?

Silver-headed, pale, tall, unworldly; my little webbed wolf-cubs, their doggy devotion. Will they, like I, always be hoping, always longing, and unable to join her in the distant sea she swims in, behind her eyes? Would she tell them the secrets her father told her? And do I, really, wish to bounce them on my sore, swollen knees, teach them to tie laces with arthritic fingers, drive them to university and say, feebly, that I used to teach at a university once, and hear them say yes, Dad, we know, and of course they would know, and I'd say I met your mother there, and they'd say, more uncomfortably this time, yes, we know, which of course they would, but I would only want to tell the story again to prove that I'd existed once, that she'd loved me, which must seem to them to be impossible. Is that true, that by then, such a thing would be impossible?

Impossible. I say it over and over, until it becomes as meaningless as a mantra. Impossible.

She's calling me from the bathroom.

Impossible.

Her wide, wet, inscrutable eyes.

Wednesday

She's quiet today. Flat and sad. Our last day. I ask her what's wrong, she says, 'Nothing,' or she says nothing. One or the other, each time I ask. She has a headache, she says. Too much wine, too much whisky. Not enough sleep. My head, too, is dull and pounding. I stare at the page and the words blur and swirl. I look up and can make out only the vaguest shape of her; I take off my glasses, but she is still little more than a smirr against the sky. Nothing is sharply defined.

I thought I saw someone out in the murk, a silver glare returned, maybe; coveting; but it was only some shadow fleeting, a flit of dark movement against the grey. When I looked again they were gone. Back to their cave, perhaps.

Mist seeping in, so the overheated cottage still is somehow chilled with damp. There isn't any sun, not even a semblance, not even a cut-out circle. The world has entirely vanished in a cloud as thick as the fog in my head. There is only a faint, shaded grey line, as if a low light shone on a piece of folded paper, sky above the crease and the pale shadow of the sea below. And I, too, am entirely lack-lustre. I haven't taken the trouble to dress, and sit in my pyjamas, robe hanging open; my hair is a rearing hedgehog, pressed sleek and flat on one side and spiny on the other; my skin is sallow as the sky, haggard and woebegone; the coffee, cold in my cup. Everything damp, and I don't know where the sun is. If asked to tell the time of day, I would say that time has ended. Soon the bland bloat moon will rise, invisible in the dank dark. I am stifling in the smell of toast and wet wool and biro ink and burnt coffee. I pull the tartan closer and try not to feel old.

She is outside on the sand. A sad slump, looking out on her last day here as if it were her last on earth.

I have little recollection, now, of how we came to be outside at midnight, in our nightclothes, by the diffuse light of a moon just one inhalation away from fullness. I recall meeting her in the doorway, emerging from her bath's mist, calling to me, laughing; saying, 'Let's dance with the selkies!' and taking my hand.

I recall her eyes, widening, wild.

I recall laughing at her as she twirled barefoot on the sands, in her nightdress; she was singing, and drinking a whisky older than she is from the bottle, and spinning, her face tilted to the fuzzy stars. Then she ran away from me as I went to her, she set off at a run towards the sea, flailing the bottle behind her for me to take, and I struggled to catch up to her and at last I caught at it and took a swig, like a teenager in a park; and when I lowered the bottle I saw she'd reached the water's edge, and she didn't hesitate, she ran right in, laughing, and then she dived under, and for a moment I couldn't see her at all, and then I saw a white billow a few yards out where she was lying upon the water. And I rushed out then into the shallows in my slippers, they are sodden, I don't remember feeling the cold, but I remember her face, I reached her and saw that she was face up and smiling, her nightdress soaked and bulging about her like a jellyfish, clinging about her hipbones, her lilac-tipped breasts. For a moment I stood and watched her, the water up to my thighs, everything restored to a tide-lapped silence after the uproar of my clumsy splashing; she seemed entirely at peace, in her element. As if she'd waded out into her nightmare and found it after all only a dream. She looked so strange and beautiful, floating pale in the moonlight, her hair sinking strand by strand as it grew heavier with the water; I don't remember how long I stood there for, wondering, entranced, but I know that at last I came to my addled senses, and scooped her out and lifted her, so light, not feeling the cold, and she clasped my neck with a shiver, laughing. I brought her in and peeled her gown from her in front of the fire. I felt a kind of freezing, shocked fury, and rubbed at her almost violently with a towel until the goose bumps at last subsided and the colour came into her cheeks. And then she looked at me contritely, child-like, and I forgave her everything, and yet tried to be a little stern: I will have no drownings, I said, however picturesque. That is what I imagine I said, wry and measured like that. And yet when I think of her lying there on the water, I start shaking, as if only now I can feel it, the cold of the sea and the thought that it might take her, and the thought that she might let it.

I carried her to the bedroom and laid her down, meaning to let her sleep.

This has all been coming back to me in fragments, through the dark brown fug of a whisky hangover.

She says she doesn't remember anything. For a moment I doubt myself: can I have dreamed it? But my soaked slippers, stuffed with newspaper, are there before the fire; her nightgown a silty, salty bundle in the sink; a glass by the chair by the window, with a drop of whisky not yet dried.

I look out at her there, and fear to take my eyes from her, and I think of her laughing, of the lightness of her, and of the gleam of her eyes, and I shake, my hands shake.

I took her to bed but I didn't let her sleep. I didn't want to let her leave me, I didn't want to let her go back under. I may have been a little rough with her; when it was over and the blood cleared from my eyes, I saw her face was once more sea-stung with tears. I brushed at her cheeks, I kissed her, I may have wept; I cannot remember ever, since I was a grown man, crying, but it comes back to me now, the salt, the shaking, the cold. A convulsion of lust, of fear. She whispered, 'Don't, don't.' Oh, my darling, I said, you can't swim! The waves will take you, if you let them, the sea can be sudden and wild. I won't let it take you. To which she replied, 'It didn't want me.' And laughed a strange laugh that sounded half a sob, and closed her eyes. And then, then I let her sleep, but I couldn't myself for thinking of her, and got up and went to my chair. I put my forehead on the cold glass of the window, rolled it from one side to the other, and realized I was looking out for her, but she was nowhere to be seen for as far as I could see along the beach. She was safe in bed sleeping, of course. I thought I saw something moving, in the moonlight, out in the water; but it was only a seal, I supposed, wondering where his new companion had gone. I felt dispirited, disturbed, by the moon, the mist. I sat at the window, pulled the blanket about me. I poured myself two fingers from the bottle beside me for warmth; the burn of it all there was to convince me it wasn't a dream (and again I feel it now in my throat and know it couldn't have been). I sat and stared at the dark and sleep seemed far away, far out in the night, withheld from me, and I watched the sea and felt the chill of it, thought of her floating there, and poured another, shaking, and maybe another, and don't remember my eyes closing. But then I heard her call me from the bedroom, and I went back to her, and found her sitting up in bed, tearful, her hair still damp and hanging in locks over her naked shoulders, shivering, and she asked where I'd been, she said she'd woken and I wasn't there. She said she'd been frightened and she'd called and called.

I couldn't sleep, I said, I'm sorry. I didn't hear you. I held her. I said, There's nothing to be frightened of. What were you frightened of? But she wouldn't answer, and could not be consoled, and sighed sorely, and swiped at her glistening dripping nose and chin, and rubbed her face sweetly on my flannelled shoulder. I soothed her until she slept but she woke again and again in the night and I soothed her, again and again. I put a hand to her head and it was moist but not hot – I feared a fever, but her skin was cold, perhaps too cold. I murmured and stroked, I whispered What's wrong, what's wrong, what frightened you, and held her and swore once more to be her barricade against that dreadful sea; I closed her poor swollen eyes with four kisses, each in turn, one eye and then the other, and again one then the other, then the cold tip of her nose and pointed chin. I stroked her hair and watched her drawn features in the dark. I watched her all night, wondering what it was that she couldn't say or speak of, what it was she'd seen; this wildness in her; thinking of her mad dance and her shivering, her body spinning and shivering, her body floating in the water, her soaked hair and skin; I thought of crossing thresholds, carrying her into my home and into this house, my wife, this girl so light in my arms. Her past, her future, and this point between, the impossibility of her presence. I watched her all night and through the dawn, and she was still there in the morning, and I was still watching over her as the sunless world at least grew lighter. And as the darkness paled, at last her face was restored to smoothness, the tears drying and leaving a salt-rime, so I imagined, upon her lashes and about the pinkish nostril-rims.

I saw her eyelids flicker and reached for her. I rolled her onto her back and held her under. Her drowning eyes. 'I have a headache,' she said, but relented in the end.

I left her sleeping again and rose to a drab day. She found me an hour later, recumbent in my chair, pallid, loitering, feeling grainy and grey with tiredness. She stood beside me and stared rather sadly at the obscure sea. I put an arm around her waist, pulling her to me, and offered to make breakfast and she turned her head away from the window with what seemed an effort, and looked at me uncomprehending for a moment, as if replaying what I'd said in order to decipher it. She seemed etiolated; her eyes bruised with purple rainclouds, the skin over her cheekbones shining as if stretched thin.

I boiled eggs and toasted bread; the first slice I cut, righting the angle left by her last, tapered to a sliver. I reserved this piece, unavoidably burnt crisp at the bottom, for myself. Such are the sacrifices I make for her. I turned, holding it up, to tell her as much, to lighten the silence, but found she had drifted out of the room. I called and she didn't come. I went into the bedroom to find her nesting at the centre of a ragged eyrie, of jumpers and socks and tights; she had pulled them around her from all corners. She was wearing one of her vastest cardigans, the sleeves flopping disconsolately from her wrists like two useless tentacles. Her head was retracted into the hooded collar, her nose and eyes peering over the wool. It seemed she was being ingested by a seaweed-green monster with toggled buttons, against which she had long since given up struggling; she was utterly forlorn, shoulders sagging, eyes mute and mournful in the depths. Are you all right? You're not ill? I said. She shook her head, mournfully, as if whatever ailed her was far worse than a sickness. 'I hate packing,' she said.

I smiled. Come on, you, I said, with forced jollity. Eggs is ready. She said, 'Oh good. Eggcellent.' This, anyway, is how I chose to hear it. That's a rather poultry pun I said, ripely. She laughed through her nose, rolled her eyes and shook her head. Humouring me. Doing her best.

At the table, she tapped the top of her egg thoughtfully, repeatedly, for longer than was necessary, before at last setting the spoon down and peeling off the fragments. Four and a half minutes, I said; again, she looked at me blankly. I boiled it for, I explained. 'Perfect,' she said, again with a forced smile. I put a hand out to her forehead, pushed her hair behind her ear gently. You're tired, I said. You didn't sleep well. 'Not really, no,' she said. I waited.

Bad dreams? I prompted, after two quiet minutes, in which she ate a toast soldier at an agonising pace, pausing after each protracted movement as if just the dip into the slowly congealing yolk were enough to exhaust her. I felt bereft. Where had she been in the night without me, what had so devastated her, that she was unwilling to volunteer? 'I don't know,' she said. 'Every time I fell asleep, I went under.' This remorseless tide in her. The sea? You were dreaming of drowning? 'No, I don't know . . . I can't remember,' she said. 'Just the sea. Black and cold.' Raven, sable, pitch, I ventured. 'Black and cold,' she said.

After another long, hollow silence, I asked, Are you okay? Not wanting to ask. She scraped at the inside of the egg without eating. Are you happy? I said, despite myself. She made a sort of moaning, sighing noise, rubbed her face with her hands, working the fingertips into her pale brows and pulling them down so the tiny line between them was pulled flat, her closed eyelids stretched. I love that tiny line, that little track of contemplation, in seminars the appearance of that line was my triumph; I cannot imagine it now, I can't think of a single intelligent thing I might have said to elicit it. She slid her hands down so that her fingers cupped her cheekbones and her palms met at her mouth, pursing it. She sat like that for a little, quiet while as I looked on, help-lessly attentive to this gesture of despair. I got up to make coffee. I'm sorry, I said, trying not to sound wretched.

'It's so early to be asking, is all,' she said. 'Am I happy, am I sad. Am I this or that. I'm not sure I'm anything before at least 11 o'clock. I just didn't sleep well, that's all. Are you making coffee? I think I'll have some.' But you don't drink coffee, I said, a little alarmed at this volte face. 'Well, never too late to try a new trick. Not an old dog yet.' And then, too brightly, as if it had occurred to her that I am just that: 'It smells delicious!' One of life's great, perpetual disappointments, I said, lugubrious, as the thing began to gurgle and spit on the stove. The taste of coffee will never live up to its fragrance. 'Oh!' she said. 'Anyway, it does smell good. It always smells bitter, when I make it.' A realization. 'It must be awful.' Oh no, I said. I relish it. You mustn't think so. And again, brightly, as I set the cup down before her and she sniffed at it, 'Delicious. You're in charge of coffee, from now on. It's my turn when it's tea.' Which of course, she over-brews, mashing the tannins out with a spoon; which of course, I didn't say. She heaped sugar in, filled the mug to the brim with milk, bent her head to sample it without lifting it from the table; put her lips out to it like some cautious proboscoid insect, sipped noisily, and smiled. 'No bad,' she said, in her best Orcadian accent. We have learned that this is the highest praise the islanders can offer. It might come to be an old joke between us, in years to come. How is the lobster, the caviar, the champagne? A solemn nod: 'No bad.' What an indulgent, epicurean marriage it seems I envisage; and how will I pay for that, on a pension? I am already resigned to the idea of my retirement, but have no notion what it might consist of or where it might take place. I have no notion of what to envisage at all, away from here, after this. After and elsewhere have become increasingly tenuous concepts. It seems somehow unlikely, somehow increasingly incredible that there is any land beyond this shore. A world of industry and administration and ordinary things. That there could be any distance greater than that between here and her, and the edge of the sea.

And yet we leave tomorrow; Mrs Odie says she has arranged for our ferryman to collect us; we are to be ready on the dock at eight o'clock. Twelve hours later, we will be back in my little sitting room. Our sitting room. The one comfy chair and the piles of papers and books. I can almost picture it; almost. I'll call for take-away and we'll drink some wine and eat pizza and we'll be married. We'll go to bed and make love and she'll sleep through the night, away from this sea, which is so black and cold. And we'll wake up and we'll be married. And every morning thereafter. For as long as we have.

Are you sad to be leaving? I asked. We can come back again, I said. For our anniversary, perhaps. Would you like that? She said, 'I don't know. Maybe. I don't know.' Let's go for a walk, I offered. Let's walk by the sea. She said, 'My head hurts.' Mine too, I said. Fresh air will do us good. Just don't let those seals lead you into a dance. I don't want you wandering off into the water. She looked at me strangely. 'Why on earth would I do that?' I can't imagine, I said.

She said, 'I might go out on my own, actually. If you don't mind. Just for a bit. I won't be long. I won't go far.' Of course, I said. Of course I don't mind. And she went.

She did warn me of this, at least, before I married her. She told me she was a solitary soul; I said I, too, am a lone wolf, but realize now that in my case this is perhaps out of happenstance, out of habit, rather than choice; that I had hoped we might be alone together. But even when she is with me and gives herself wholly, she seems at the same moment to slip free. This ache of the space between us, which I can only fill with desire, which only aches because of it, because I want so much to own just some small part of her, for a moment, entirely. I sometimes think I know nothing at all about her. And sometimes I think there is some particular thing that I will never know, that I can never hope to know, for all my probing.

Her shoes and socks make a little mound behind her on the beach. She's been staring out for hours, and I, within, go on staring out at her. Just as it has been since we came here. My young wife on the shore. I should go to her; I don't know what it is that prevents me.

Tomorrow we leave; what will she do, without the sea to watch, without the sound of it? What will she do with all her hours? How will she sleep, what will she dream?

The mist is thinning, lifting off the sea and brightening, or perhaps we are drifting clear of it.

She stands at the tide-mark and does not draw back from it. It laps at her toes and she allows it, allows the sea to kiss her bare feet without disdain; and it flows over the fine bird-bones of her toes, her rough torn toenails with their chipped paint, and up to the sharp jab of her ankles. She gasps silently, holding her breath.

No, of course I could not know this, she is too far from me to hear that tiny intake. And yet I think I do.

A silvery path shimmers into being on the water like a spell; it shivers up the beach, picking out the glitter of scattered stones and winkle-shells, all the way to her feet. She takes a hesitant step forward. She walks the silvered path out from the water's edge; I should go to her, I should hold her, I should hold her back, but don't; I find myself paralysed, fascinated, unable to move as I wait to see what she will do; I can only stand by helpless and watch, unable to turn away from her even for a second, powerless behind the window. She stops in the shallows, the water almost to her knees, and I can only will her not to go on, the sea silver all around her, my hands against the glass pressing out to her and she goes no further for a minute, for two, she goes no further and I let out a breath I hadn't known I was holding, and it steams the glass and when I swipe it away I see that she is squatting, now, her skirt hitched up and trailing, and she is reaching her hands out; I can do nothing but watch as she plunges them into the silver, she splashes her face with the pearly water, she pulls her hands back over her hair; she crouches there now, hands splayed before her as if waiting for a transformation. She stands.

The illusion folds. The silver fades back to grey. There's a transparency to her; I can almost see through her, to nothing. I breathe her name and she vanishes behind it.

She doesn't hear. I trace her name in the mist of my breath but it's gone before I can reach the last letter, and there she still stands.

I should go to her, now.

*

I sit down on the rocks and watch; I pull off my shoes and unroll my socks; neat, ribbed, navy-blue, pulled up the calf without a wrinkle, I unroll them and neatly turn them together in a ball and, standing, pocket them, and step onto the sand. It is unexpectedly sharp, each tiny rock-shard not quite smoothed enough; and it is saturated with seawater that is very, very cold. I have almost reached her, almost. I approach quietly, not wishing to startle her, as if she is an animal that might take fright and bolt. The water comes for my toes, a thousand freezing needles, but soon I feel nothing; standing ankle-deep beside her, all I can feel is a numbed tingle, and I am conscious of how pale and gnarled my feet are, of the black hair on the knuckles, they are flattened and fattened in the water like another, dead man's, feet, the big old horned toenail, bent inward, a yellowed claw. Monster's feet, which shouldn't be on show. Monster's feet and monster's hands, I have.

She looks out to sea, puts the tips of her thumbs to the tips of her forefingers to make a frame. A photograph. 'We've been here twelve days,' she says, not to me, staring out. So little, so long? It seems only a moment, it seems forever. Green light through the trees, wine in the garden; our wedding day, the sun pale in her hair and the falling leaves: impossible. I cannot reach beyond this horizon.

'Look,' she says suddenly. 'Look at the birds, look at them circling.' Wheeling, spiralling. Crying 'look-away', it sounds like, I say. They pour away from the sky, diving, and as I watch, the world tilts. Look-away. She doesn't.

'Richard . . .' she says. 'What if we . . .' And trails off, like that, a silver tail evading capture. What if we what? I ask; she doesn't answer. What if we stay here, does she mean to say, as her eyes do? What if we don't go home? What if we run into the sea, now?

What if we drown? What if we die? We won't drown, I want to say. We won't die. But I will.

What if we what?

We sit together on the sand and watch the sun fall. We have been sitting for what seems a long time. The light shifting; her eyes suddenly veiled, just as suddenly shimmering. Luminous, obscure. I no longer feel the cold; my bones are numb.

Out where the sea meets the sky, a swelling of deep, powdery purple cloud, a band of palest eau-de-nil below, and then the reflection of the cloud again purpling the sea violet. The colour of your birthmark, I say; 'and my bruises,' she smiles.

Above the cloud bank . . . 'Periwinkle,' she says. 'I had a crayon by that name, as a child.' Me, too, I say. How extraordinary. We fall quiet again.

The evening deepens. The cloud breaks across a full moon.

Mauve, now, I say.

Minutes pass, the night cools; I put an arm around her, she shivers and winches herself into my side. We don't go in. An hour passes, an age of peace. We watch the day end.

Tyrolean purple, I offer; it is almost entirely dark. I am almost near her, now. 'Indigo,' she says, softly, so as not to stir the silence.

'Prussian blue.' Indian ink. 'Mussel-blue. Midnight blue.' Not quite, I say. But come. Let's go in. 'Bedtime blue,' she sighs.

*

The night is so dense that there's nothing to see of it, just black, just darkness without, and silence within, but for the sound of the wind, and our breathing, slowing. She is almost inaudible. I can still hear her last gasp, the last sound before this silence; I can almost still feel her around me.

What if we stayed here? I whisper. Thee and me. She doesn't say anything. Perhaps she is sleeping. But I think she smiles, in the dark.

She walks into the sea, leaving the faintest swirl in the fog, the water barely eddying around her, and I cry out, I cannot make a sound, I cry out in silence, Oh, do not go on; the echo of some ancient warning of which all but this is lost, do not walk on, do not go on; I cry out, silent, frozen by the fog, I cry out from the beach and the waters close over her and she is lost to the world below, her hair floating out among the shifting fronds and wrapped around by tendrils, by tentacles, pulled down into the murk, all the lost souls stretching pale arms from the gloom to greet her and pull her under and bind her in the dark green weed; her hair floating out and turning to wrack, her pale skin pearling, her eyes become bottle-glass smoothed by the sands and on, into the deep, into the dark, dissipating, oh do not go on, do not go in, do not go under, do not go on, I weep and I wake, weeping, and I try to hold her, I reach for her and she

Thursday

When I woke this morning she was gone.

I had set an alarm for seven. I woke at five from a heavy, reeling, pressing sleep, and she was gone. I reached for her, I called for her, and had no answer; the blind was open, the moon was full, almost touching the water, casting its silver path. The sky clear. She did not dance on the silvered beach. Everything as bright and sharp and heightened as a hallucination. I listened to the sea Shhh and slept and dreamed she was taken from me, dreamed she was gone, and woke and she was gone. I thought I heard her gasp but she was gone and when I called her name she didn't answer.

I call again; there is no answer.

I can't see her on the beach; we are due to leave at nine and there is no sign of her, and everything she's brought is still strewn about the floor; I throw jumpers and jeans and socks at the open bag and stuff it all in and call again but no answer. Her handbag is still here, she can't have gone far. As usual, no reception. Out on the path, out in the wind

Nothing.

No answer at Mrs Odie's.

Nowhere to be seen on the beach.

*

I seek her footsteps, I scour the sand for traces, and there are none. I sift it through my hands and find nothing, nothing but shards of dead shells, I can't feel my fingers, I am numb, numb.

I climb up the rocks, I slipper and slide over the rocks, calling out. There is no answer.

*

Nine o'clock has come and gone; from the rocks I watched the ferryman arrive at the dock, I watched him waiting, I saw him leave the boat and stalk up the beach and knock at the door and knock again and he came around to the front and glowered through the windows but there was no one home. I called out to him but he didn't hear, and I couldn't in any case think what to say. He couldn't wait indefinitely. He went back to his boat and sailed off into the late dawn. The boat is gone, without us.

She is gone.

Blood thudding in my temples like the tide around an empty cavern.

*

Midday has come and gone. There is no one on the beach or on the cliffs. It is bright, bright and cruelly clear. To the south, our plane will be leaving its flare across the sky.

I look out to sea; there is nothing. No silver selkies at play. No song that I can hear.

The gulls wheeling, crying, 'Look-away, look-away.'

I cry out to her on the beach and strain to hear her returning call.

No answer.

*

At Mr Begg's the ting of the bell jangles my nerves and I stand stupidly amid the limp produce and the turnips and the sweets, and Mr Begg asks if I'm looking for anything in particular and I laugh a high strange laugh and say I'm looking for my wife, he hasn't seen her? He'll let me know if he does? He raises his eyebrows and nods 'aye'.

At the hotel, the lounge is empty and horribly quiet and dusty in the daylight. It's too early for the barmaid to be around, and Bob and Linda and Mart and Will are of course long gone. The hotel receptionist comes to the bar and can't help me; having never met me or my wife how could she, why should she; her expression remains carefully impassive as I order a whisky; she checks the clock indiscreetly, but it has gone midday and she pours it without comment and I gulp it down and ask for another and then wander out into the wind, calling.

*

I pound on the door of the old croft house, I peer in the window. I pound on the window but the old man has left, or is hiding. Tins and beer cans litter the carpet but the filthy bedding is gone. I shall have no answer from Old Tom.

*

The ruined church stands hollow to the sky; no echo of her pledge remains. No one hides among the headstones, and I slump among them and listen at the ground but the old dead keep silent and there is only the sound of the gulls.

*

I circle all the island round, and cannot find her. I call on beach and rock and cliff, and cannot find her. I peer into the caverns, I call from the heights, I bellow on the highest crag and the sea rushes below me, and I hear only her name echoed back, empty. And the crabs edge off sideways, telling no tales, and the sorrowful seals tell no secrets. And the sky lowers, closing in.

*

The sun has set, the full moon rising. She is not here to dance under it. No, I am wrong, tonight the moon is waning. A day has passed.

It will be days, weeks, before it is full again.

I pour myself whisky and wait for the morning.

Friday

I have sat all night in the chair by the window and barely slept; I drifted under and woke all through the night and called again and again, hearing her name over and over, every time, the wrench of remembering, and the strangeness of the sound in the silence echoing so that I am unsure now if I spoke aloud; once I thought I heard her say, I'm here, Richard. But I can't be sure of that either. I poured whisky. The familiar burn.

Watching from the window, watching the empty beach, the moonlight made my empty mind ache, pressing upon my eyelids; I let them close and thought I saw her, walking into the water, dancing, white arms reaching and her voice calling, singing, and I would gladly have gone to her, gone out to her there in the water to be pulled under, and I called her name, and it woke me, my own voice, reedy in the thinned-out silence. I would exchange anything for a last spell to wake me, but I know it is not a dream. So instead I want a spell to let me sleep a long, unbroken, deceived sleep in which she is not gone. I can only drowse and I fight against the tide because when I slip under I watch her walk again and again into the sea, and now the sky is lightening and still there is no sign.

It's cold. A drop more. The last of it.

*

A shake of the shoulder woke me, and I grasped at the hand for a moment like a drowning man. But looking up through the blear I saw no one, and realized it was only a shiver, and could have wept, if I wasn't sobbing already.

I called out, called her phone, called for her on the beach; no answer. Tried Mrs Odie. No answer.

I called the police. I said to the officer who answered, I can't find my wife. She's gone, I explained. I have made myself a cup of tea, while I wait for him to arrive. It is going cold.

My wretched heart is beating so hard and dull that it hurts.

*

The policeman, out of his depth, performing a role, wants to know when I last saw her. He wants to know how long we've been married. Two weeks, I say. Two weeks today. I try not to cry, remembering her, in her wedding gown, in her nightgown, silk, her skin. He wants to know if there's anywhere I can think of, that she might have gone to. He wants a description. I find I cannot give one. I have no photograph. I say, she is tall, she is thin, she has white hair and green, or bluish, or grey eyes. What am I to tell him? She has a violet freckle on her hipbone, a bruise; her hands and toes are webbed and the veins behind her knees are green. These few meagre secrets – haven't I a right to them? He asks to see our bedroom, he looks through her things. She has left a book behind, an Orkney poet. No clues to be found. She has made no mark, no scribbles in the margins. This book might have belonged to anyone.

She has left her coat too, waxy, briny from her days on the beach. There is nothing to identify her in the pockets, or in her abandoned bag; just a pencil and a sketchpad, a single portrait of me, fire lit, glowering, and page upon page that I did not see her drawing of underwater currents swirling, sea-stained, heavy and shining with graphite; it comes off on my fingers and everything

I touch is smeared with it. The hollows of my eyes are rubbed with it, like a highwayman. Her phone was buried at the bottom, among the sand, the shells, the stubs of pencil. It was switched off. There are no numbers saved, apart from mine.

He asks after Mrs Odie and I say I can't get hold of her. He says that's no like her. She's mibbe off seeing her sister in Inverness, he says. I nod. I don't know what to tell him. He wants to know if we can contact my wife's family. I say, I don't know her family. I don't know where to look. I think her father is dead. And somehow I don't even plead with him, I can't even ask him to find her for me, I don't see how he can, when I have never known myself how to find her. Anyway he says he'll try to. He asks, how was her mood, the day before she . . . ? Did she seem upset; did she seem strange in any way? I almost laugh. She seemed strange in every way, I want to tell him. I can give you no account of her moods. This sky of yours, this sea, that is how she seemed – like that, like the light changing. You tell me, if you know what the weather will do.

I say only, she was sad to be leaving. She liked it here. He tells me to stay on the island while he makes enquiries. He looks at me closely as if waiting for a reaction. He will be back, he says. I mustn't leave. As if I could.

*

I found the red lipstick in her bag, too, and put some on, a synthetic waxy kiss, to touch where her lips touched. After the policeman was gone, of course. It leaves a mark on my whisky glass, as if she has just stolen a sip.

Her answerphone message is pre-recorded, with a gap for her name; I have listened over and over to her saying it in that gap, in barely a whisper, so I have to strain to hear it at all. She has already recorded her new surname. Her married name. When did she do this? There are twenty-seven voicemail messages. I listen to them all. I listen to myself: anxious, wheedling, pleading; a slur, barely an aspiration, an empty sound. I listen to myself breathing, I catch the fragment of a sigh. A sob, a dreadful rattle, a rasp. I say her name. I listen to myself, yesterday, last night, this morning, saying her name.

*

Mr Begg serves me a bottle of whisky with a hard sympathy. I buy the best and don't care for the cost. To appease him maybe.

I buy cigarettes and smoke the whole pack without noticing.

I buy bread and slice it in wedges and burn it under the grill on purpose, and the smell brings tears to my eyes but I have to eat something.

*

I wander the house; she goes out as I enter. Echoes, traces; her bright hair like cobwebs left in corners. Not enough to weave a bracelet of. I curl up under her coat and try to smell her through the smell of the sea; beneath the rime and seaweed, the deep salt-water smell. I catch it in the air and think that she's come through the door, think she's behind me when it is only some shift in the tide or the wind. I pour salt into the palm of my hand and touch my tongue to it and can't seem to taste it. There, on the sill, are the pebbles she placed in a ring; and the urchin skeleton, the paperweight stone, the hollow bone, all piled neatly in their cairn. A broken pile of tesserae that refuse to tessellate. I scatter them, and sit among them in the silence after their clatter, trying not to listen to the useless Shhh-shh of the sea.

I prowl through the rooms and find nothing to tear, nothing to rip and gouge at. I yowl and gnash. I see myself enraged, filling this little room with my bulk, preposterous and horrifying, black-furred, swiping about me so the walls are torn by my claws, the rug ripped under them, fibres and fragments of wool, paper, tartan, glass and slate and china flying; the ornaments dashed from the mantel and smashed; leaving spittle and tatters in the wake of my fury, snarling, everything laid bare, stripped to plaster and stone and bone – nothing left of her at all . . .

Horrible. A dram, to steady the nerves.

It chinks against the glass. A death at sea. Hold the bottle straight.

I press my head to the window, and scan the beach.

I thought I saw, for a moment, something out in the water, a familiar flash of something surface and dive beneath the low waves, rippling on the sheeny sand.

But now the sea is perfectly still, all passion spent.

This grey place. Everything grey. Oyster, dove's wing, silver . . . Grey. Everything ashes and bone, drained, nothing, neither night nor sunlight, nothing, nothing.

I look out, at the sea, at the gulls, the deranged sky, the clouds ripping in the wind. I look down at her cairn of stones; I do not recall the patient hour I must have spent in reassembling it.

My fingers, I notice, have turned slightly blue in the cold. I clutch my glass.

It's getting dark again and I try to doze but I can't. I dream her dreams.

The wind cracks and shudders.

I am jolted by a bang at the door but there is no one.

I thought I heard her say my name.

Saturday

People out on the cliffs this morning in bright fluorescent windcheaters, swinging torch beams into the dark caves. It is too dangerous, I'm told, for me to join them. If they call out to each other, I can't hear them for the wind, and she won't either.

The policeman comes by to deliver no news. He asks questions I can't answer, and leaves seeming defeated. I am not to leave the island. He says he will be back.

I try to read but can't make my eyes focus for sleep or whisky or tears. I go through my notes and shuffle my index cards and can find neither purpose nor meaning. These men bewitched and bereft; they sicken me. This grand anthology, my gift to posterity . . . I have nothing more to say on the matter.

One by one I feed my pages to the fire, and by their light I read the book that she was reading:

> *A stranger came in*
> *So beautiful*
> *She seemed to be a woman from the sea*

Perhaps one day she'll walk in, calmly, soaked to the skin and dripping, hair in wet ropes and streaming, and she'll sit down in the corner as if there is nothing amiss at all. The latch lifts

No.

I take her place on the beach and imagine her watching me, from the window, as if we've changed places, but I turn and there is no one there, there is only an empty, blank hole. Nothing within, and nothing beyond. All I can make out is the reflection of the sea.

I watch its shifts and changes. It is powder-blue, it is amethyst, it is black, bruised, blood-purple, garnet; calm and flat, harmless, or biding its time. It is a clear night, tonight. The soft dimming into evening; all the old, dead ghosts of stars, haunting the clear sky, brightening against the dark in the glimmerans. Lovely islanders' word for twilight. How she'd love that. Or was it her I had it from?

The sky periwinkle, with a sketching of graphite clouds, the barest pencil-trace; lilac where it meets the sea, deepening up to the apex, mussel-blue. That was hers. I am trying to hear her voice say it. Prussian blue. Ink-washed. Indigo. Lovely, hollow words, without her. Bedtime blue, Richard, she says. Bedtime blue.

I stand in numb bare feet, the cold gnarling the swollen joints, and I think of swimming out but the water is bitterly cold and I quail at it, I haven't the heart, the courage to go in, to go under.

I'm sorry, I say.

All I have left is this act of empty rhetoric, this endless address to an absence. What if we . . . ? I try to recall a single conversation with clarity and cannot. I cannot remember the last thing she said, what it was that she murmured to me or to the night. The last time we made love, she was already vanishing, slipping from me, dissipating.

I can almost, almost recall the salt of her skin. Her gasp, her last gasp.

Perhaps there is nothing left of her but an old man's sigh.

The searchers' torches have been extinguished for the night, the caves left to their darkness. The tide is close. The beach is empty. I don't think, tonight, that she'll swim out of the water in her pale skin. I am cold, shaking. I must go in.

*

Burnt toast and whisky. How long should I wait – for nine days to pass, for a full moon? In a year and a day will I still be here watching? There is nothing to go home for. I could go back to my work, after all, and bury myself, and try not to hear the curious gossip, the laughter, or even worse the pity; no, I don't think I can.

At some point I will have to write to them, and resign. Or perhaps I won't bother. I wonder how long it will take them to notice that I'm not there, how much longer to give me up. Eventually I suppose they'll clear out the office, box up the books that I can see no further use for, haul the desk out through the narrow door.

I have no place there. I am a cancelled man. I cannot see what I should do with the days ahead; I cannot see tomorrow morning even. Taking the ferry, the plane, the train, and coming back to my house in the darkness and sitting in my one comfy chair and festering, hoping she'll return, if nothing else to retrieve her bags, that sorry pile still sitting, presumably, on the living room floor. I shall hold them hostage, I shall wait for her to come and collect her books, all scrawled in the margin with her marks; I shall try to decipher the message there, I shall try to follow the scroll of her thought. But perhaps the pages when I turn them will all be unmarked, like the book she left behind her, or blank altogether, white and silent; or perhaps I'll find the bags filled with nothing but wrack and sand.

The wind in the flue. The fire has gone out.

I have found at last a mark in that book of hers, a last blue line of biro underlining. It is just this: 'Best leave the paper blank.'

Acknowledgments

Thank you to my excellent editor Laura Barber for her sympathetic and intelligent reading, and my agent Jenny Hewson for her understanding, reassurance and patience; and to all at RCW and at Granta.

Catherine, David, Jonathan, Patrick, Ruby, Francis, Gemma, and Justin, thank you for reading fragments of this over the past few years and for all your perceptive comments. Scarlett Thomas and Rod Edmond, who read an early complete draft and asked some very useful questions, as well as saying some lovely things – thank you both.

The Arts Council of England kindly awarded a small grant to enable me to travel to the beautiful Orkney island of Westray and to spend some time writing this book.

Thank you to my wonderful family, especially my loving parents, grandmother Nancy, and brilliant sister Lucy. Thank you to the Thorpe family for their support. And thank you Ali for listening, and giving me space and time to work, and much else besides.